# The Omega File

Special Agent O'Malley, FBI

By

Colin Setterfield

ISBN 978-1-988719-12-2

# Contents

1.  PROLOGUE

2.  Early Sunday Morning

3.  Hemlock Under Siege

4.  Special Agent O'Malley

5.  The Groom Lake Base

6.  RC-HGH

7.  An Interesting Correlation

8.  The Base Security

9.  Exploring the Correlation

10. The General and his Goon

11. More about that correlation

12. The Agents plan ahead

13. A Quick visit to Hemlock

14. A visit to the Field Hospital

15. Spilled Milk

16. The Cranwell Brothers

17. O'Malley and Tam

18. Sheriff Cranwell

19. Back at the Hotel

20. Blake in Trouble Again.

21. Returning to Area 51

22. O'Malley's Discovery

23. Searching for an Ally

24. The Palm Palace Bar

25. About that Ally

26. A Heart to Heart

27. Breaking in Again

28. Clandecker and Shaw

29. O'Malley and Tam on Level 3

30. Cactus Station

31. Arrival of the Bases Security

32. Trapped

33. A Shock for the Sheriff.

34. Epilogue

More books by Colin Setterfield

# PROLOGUE

The small town of Hemlock, Lincoln County, nestled between several hillocks of the Nevada desert's dry, dusty terrain. Mining of industrial minerals played a huge role in the area and the many farm mines provided the owners with extra income. In Hemlock, four medium sized hotels accommodated hikers, writers, sensation seekers and science fiction enthusiasts, all after one prize: stories of aliens and secret military projects. Hemlock rested in the foothills of the Groom Lake Mountain range, about twenty-five miles North of Area 51, the most secretive military site in the world.

The local population of two thousand people could swell to as many as three-thousand when Hemlock's tourist committee advertised the usual summer specials for UFO enthusiasts and sensation-seekers. The hotels and RV parks provided attractive accommodation deals, supplemented with specialized guided tours in the Groom Mountains, which provided the occasional opportunity to view the military base. The town's law-enforcement consisted of a single office and cell, with one police officer on duty, Sheriff Mortimer Cranwell. He kept the local population under strict scrutiny and made sure that the UFO enthusiasts understood the military base's many security requirements.

Mortimer's Great grandfather, purchased the original farm in 1921 and one could say the Cranwell family owned the town of Hemlock. Industrial Minerals, mined in the area for thirty years before the U.S. military took over the area, created a measure of profit for the Cranwell family before it became a test site for some of the world's most advanced military innovations. Area 51's mysterious reputation helped the Cranwell's mining business and farm operation, to morph into a small town with a tourist-driven economy.

Over time, tensions developed between the base's personnel and the many sensation-seekers from Hemlock. Security became a top priority and tourists were often arrested when they got too close to the military operation. Feelings between the base and Hemlock's municipal office personnel would run high at such times but usually settled down at the end of each tourist season. Hemlock's problems, however, were about to take a dramatic turn.

***

# 1

## Early Sunday Morning

In the early hours of Sunday morning, a strange sound woke Sheriff Mortimer Cranwell from a deep sleep. The Cranwell home overlooked the small town of Hemlock, but despite the abode's raised elevation, noise seldom ever reached their bedroom. It appeared to be a vehicle at speed, on its way to the center of town. A vehicle at night, and at speed, seemed odd.

"What's up, darling?" His wife of fifteen years sat up on the bed and leaned over to switch on the bedside lamp.

"Nothing, honey—I heard a noise. It appears to be a vehicle driving through the center of town."

Cranwell got out of bed and went to the window. The sound of the vehicle's engine diminished as it left the town's perimeter until he could no longer hear it. The sheriff yawned and went back to bed.

His wife turned over to face him. "Did you see anything? What was it?"

"Nothing to worry about—turn off the light and let's go back to sleep." He glanced at the bedside clock: 4:00 a.m.

She turned off the light, snuggled up to him and they both fell asleep within minutes.

*

Early Monday morning sheriff Cranwell made his way down to the small law-enforcement office in Roswell Avenue. It would be another hour before the town came to life so he settled down behind his desk and turned on the computer. A quick glance at the weather confirmed a sunny day with a high of 85 degrees and no clouds. It would be an ideal day for a hike in the mountains, or to view the Groom Lake base from a distance.

A cup of coffee became the next priority and he made his way into the kitchenette beside the cell. The small jail cell seldom ever got used. The occasional bar fight plus the few reports of stolen property, featured amongst Hemlock's most heinous of crimes and the low criminal element made the sheriff's job a peaceful one. Whenever he needed to run trouble-makers out of town, his brother, Charles, would back him up.

A knock on the office door drew Cranwell's attention away from the coffee.

"Coming," he shouted. He poured a mug of coffee and set it down on his desk. The knock became more insistent.

He frowned. "Hold your horses, I said I'm coming."

He slipped off the inside lock and yanked the door open. The manager of the largest hotel, the Sunset Rest, stood there with an expression of concern on his face.

"I have three very sick people, Morty. I can't raise Bill Griffin and I need to get them into the clinic as quickly as possible."

"Did you try Bill's home?" Cranwell asked.

"Yes, but he isn't answering his phone or the doorbell. He normally has Florence Blunt as the alternative. When she's on duty her name would be written on the board outside the clinic door, but there's nothing—no forwarding number on the voicemail either."

"Florence is attending a seminar in Vegas this week and Bill is supposed to be manning the clinic. How sick are these people you're talking about?"

"I haven't a clue what's wrong with them. They seem to be suffering some sort of poisoning, but it's difficult to say. I can't smell any alcohol so they aren't drunk or suffering from hangovers."

"Where are they, now?"

"Sitting in my SUV."

Cranwell thought for a moment. "I'll go and see what's happened to Bill. Take the patients back to the clinic and wait there for me."

Cranwell jumped into his pickup and drove to Bill Griffin's house. Griffin, a retired paramedic ran the small clinic but referred any serious medical problems to Las Vegas. Cranwell's brother, Charles, possessed a helicopter pilot's license and emergency victims could be airlifted to the hospital in Vegas. Such an occurrence would be a rare event in Hemlock. The small, two-seater chopper remained parked in the corner of the local sports field and Charles often used it to take sightseers up into the Groom Mountain range, however, a no-fly zone existed over most of Area 51. Mortimer could remember two occasions when a resident or tourist contracted a serious, life-threatening condition, which necessitated an airlift to the hospital.

On arrival at Griffin's home Cranwell went to the door and rang the bell. When he received no answer he checked around the back of the house and then the car garage. The back of Griffin's Jeep stuck out beyond the end of the adjacent carport and Cranwell thought it odd for Bill to be so sound asleep, that he would not hear the doorbell. He returned to the front of the abode and held his finger to the bell for ten seconds. When the action drew no response he became concerned.

A quick glance through the living room window revealed nothing out of the ordinary. He shouted Bill's name and banged on the door several times but got no response. There appeared no other way to wake the paramedic up so he broke a glass panel in the door and released the lock. A quick look in the kitchen produced no one and the second bedroom, off the hallway, came up empty. Bill, a widower, stayed alone and sometimes rented a room out to tourists when the hotels were full, but the house appeared to be unoccupied.

The main bathroom also produced zero sign of any life, which left the main bedroom and en-suite bathroom, for a final search. The sheriff entered the bedroom and at first saw no one until his eye caught a foot on the floor, which stuck out beyond the bed. The paramedic lay on the floor by the open window. Cranwell knelt down and turned the man over onto his back. The vacant eyes stared up at him and some spittle dribbled from the half-open mouth.

"Bill—can you hear me?" Shouted Cranwell.

He felt for a pulse and discovered a weak flutter; Bill still hung onto life.

He stood up, pulled a phone from his pocket and called his brother.

Charles Cranwell's sleepy voice answered. "What's up bro?"

"Charles? Something bad has happened in our town."

"What're you talking about, Morty? Nothing bad ever happens here."

Cranwell explained the situation with Bill and the three patients at the clinic. "There are too many to transport in the chopper. I don't have enough medical experience to help any of them and I can't revive Bill. We need help right away."

Charles became silent for a moment and then came up with an idea. "I'll make an inquiry to see if there isn't a doctor at the Groom Lake base. It would take too long for me to fly the people to Vegas, anyway—I have a contact at the Pentagon who may be able to give me the base commander's number."

Mortimer countered. "We've never spoken to anyone at the Base. Nobody even knows who's in charge—they aren't likely to lend us a helping hand since Hemlock's such a thorn in their side."

"Relax, Morty. I think they would be only too eager to help and have us owe them one."

"I'll get hold of my pal to find out who should be contacted. I think it will be the quickest way to get help for these people," Charles retorted.

Mortimer didn't like the suggestion. "I would hate to owe the military anything, but a death in Hemlock for reasons unknown is the worst advertisement for our local business."

"We'll have to deal with it, Morty," Charles answered."

The sheriff gave in. "Okay. I'll see if I can find the clinic's keys and move Bill down there."

Problems of this nature never occurred in Hemlock. Five years prior, a tourist on return from a hike in the mountains, discovered a trove of military ordinance, hidden in a cave. News of the discovery caused a drop-off in sightseers for several months and Hemlock's small economy suffered the consequence. The local business owners struggled along, but after several months the situation returned to normal.

Over the years the Cranwell brothers sold off the residential properties to the people who owned the few small businesses in the town, but the brothers held the deeds to all commercial buildings and rented each premises, to its respective business owner. The brothers also owned the hotels, which made a reasonable annual profit from all the tourists and sensation seekers. Due to the fall-off of the Cranwell Mine production over the years, Charles sold some of the miner's homes to the more regular UFO enthusiasts, who lived in Vegas.

Sheriff Cranwell grabbed the stricken paramedic's shoulders and managed to prop him up, with his back against the bed. Whatever sickness plagued Bill Griffin overcame him prior to bedtime on the previous evening—he still wore his clothes.

Mortimer went into the kitchen and spied the clinic's keys on a hook behind the door. With the keys tucked into his pocket Cranwell opened the front door and dragged the unconscious form through the hall entrance and to the front steps of the front porch. He used the steps to get beneath the clinic manager's body and drape it over his shoulders. Ten minutes later he drove into the clinic's driveway and parked close to the front entrance.

The hotel manager leaped out of his vehicle to give a hand and minutes later, Charles Cranwell arrived. Together they lifted Bill Griffin out of the pickup and carried him into the clinic, a converted house. The three able-bodied men then assisted the sick tourists out of the manager's SUV and deposited them on the sofa in the waiting room. The tourists were able to make their way with a little help and each appeared to be in great distress.

"My contact at the Pentagon knew exactly who to call. I have organized a doctor from the Groom Lake facility—he'll be here in about thirty minutes. A military chopper was available to fly him in," said Charles.

"I'll drive to the sports field. That's where they'll land," said Mortimer. He jumped into his pickup and zoomed off.

Thirty minutes later he returned with the doctor and a military medic. The doctor examined each patient with care.

"I can't pinpoint any particular thing, other than they all seem to be suffering from a similar malady. It could be food poisoning, or something similar. We need to get them to Vegas immediately."

Ж

# 2

## Hemlock Under Siege

The four patients were ferried to the Groom Lake Base airfield and airlifted by military helicopter to the Las Vegas general hospital. On return to Hemlock, the Cranwell brothers found another group of people gathered outside the clinic. Some manifested signs of illness, but those who brought them appeared to be fine. The strange sickness did not seem to target everyone and as head of law enforcement in Hemlock, Mortimer felt a huge responsibility to solve the mystery.

He still possessed the doctor's cell number should any further developments take place and he made the call to report the latest event and ask for a bus which could be used to pick the people up from the clinic and ferry them to the base airfield for evacuation. In due course, a bus arrived from Area 51 to collect all the sick. Mortimer received further bad news later that afternoon—the death of Bill Griffin, along with ten other patients. Medical experts at the hospital appeared to be at a loss as to the real underlying cause. Analysts claimed each patient suffered a massive failure of internal organs but could find no trace of a virus, or poison. The onset of the sickness emerged as a sudden loss of energy, followed by internal pains. It appeared as though a foreign body entered the victim's system and then disappeared without a trace.

The Cranwell's were informed that a delegation of medical investigators would be flown into Groom Lake the next day, and bussed to Hemlock. The lead investigator, a medical scientist by the name of Dr. Tobias, asked for samples from the water supply to be taken and a closure of the supermarket. He also requested that the two small eating houses be shut down, prior to their arrival, plus the closure of the hotels. A state of emergency existed in Hemlock. That is when the rumors started.

Sheriff Cranwell received several calls from local residents, with regard to a strange event which took place in the early hours of Sunday morning—they all heard a vehicle travel through the town center at speed. Many of the tourists, booked into the hotels and RV parks, blamed the whole advent on an alien presence. Mortimer called his brother, Charles.

"I personally heard a vehicle travel through the town center in the early hours of Sunday morning. You know how sound travels at night—it woke me up," said Mortimer.

"There's no evidence of anyone having committed an act of terrorism. The vehicle you heard could have been anyone out on an early morning jaunt, or be leaving Hemlock. Have you checked with the hotels?"

The sheriff became indignant. "Of course I've checked with the hotels and the RV parks. Nobody appears to have left the town in the early hours of Sunday morning. Do you think I'm dumb, bro?"

"Hold your horses, Morty. I didn't say you were dumb. We just need to cover all the bases. Right now we can't connect your early-morning vehicle to the sudden deaths."

"Many of the visitors are saying it's an alien invasion," said Mortimer.

"We don't believe in all that hooey about UFO's and aliens—unless you've changed your mind," Charles responded.

Mortimer sounded conflicted. "I don't believe in aliens, but I'm telling you I personally woke up that morning and went to the window to have look.

I heard a powerful engine, like a four-by-four, speeding down the main drag. It finally disappeared out of earshot in the direction of the base."

Charles's voice contained a measure of skepticism. "Did you have anything to drink before going to bed?"

Mortimer reacted with anger. "Only my usual nightcap. You know I'm not a drunk."

Charles returned to placation mode. "Relax, bro. I was just asking, and I didn't say you were drunk. It certainly doesn't sound like a UFO problem to me—just someone leaving town in the middle of the night."

"Maybe. But it's strange that it coincides with everyone getting sick."

"We'll see what the experts say tomorrow when they've had a chance to investigate," said Charles.

*

Rumors with regard to the presence of aliens in the area tended to generate good business for Hemlock. Area 51's reputation added a mysterious element to the Groom Lake base and it came to be known by many different names, since its establishment in the mid-20th century. Names, such as the "Dreamland Resort," and "Paradise Ranch" have been past labels for the best-defended enterprise in human history—also, perhaps, the military's worst kept secret. No one knew who directed the business of the Groom Lake base—any contact with its top-brass took place through a second party. Officially, the Pentagon claimed to provide the mandate for projects run at the base but many thought the CIA called the shots. The Nellis Air Force Range and the Nevada Test Site came as an addition to the World War Two effort when the U.S. found a need to develop nuclear weapons and specialized spy planes.

In the initial establishment of Hemlock, the town's close proximity to the test site caused a few problems between the two parties. Some experts said the presence of radiation fallout in the area from nuclear tests, long gone, could still endanger the lives of the town's residents and its tourist trade. A committee of nuclear experts dispelled the notion, however. They maintained there would be nothing for the town's folk to fear. Concerns of potential radiation sickness from the early nuclear tests hindered the initial establishment of Hemlock, but these no longer existed—no one had ever contracted radiation sickness.

The Military did, however, object to Hemlock's close proximity to the Base's secret weapon's development initiative. They cited possible security problems, but the Cranwell enterprise provided little for them to contest from a legal standpoint. An uneasy truce, based on the mutual aspirations of both communities, led to an eventual practice of manageable cohabitation.

*

The next day a team of experts arrived from Vegas, to start a thorough investigation of the causes. The single main road saw a train of vehicles on their way out of town. Every visitor beat a hasty retreat lest the sickness befell them. Charles Cranwell informed everyone to consult a local physician on their return home. With a collapse of Hemlock's tourist industry imminent the hotels made promises of extra special rates to motivate the return of the people at a later date. When the final all-clear came from the sheriff, the town's local enterprise would breathe a sigh of relief.

Dr. Alec Tobias, a forensic scientist, led the team of five investigators and they all spent the day in the examination of every possible cause that might have contributed to the event. The food at the hotel, eating houses and pub, the supplies in the supermarket and the water supply—all came up clean. At the end of the first day, the Cranwell brothers felt frustrated and at their wit's end. News from Las Vegas General Hospital spelled out more bad news—the death of the remainder of the patients.

"It's like a thief came in overnight, sowed the bad seed and left the following morning," said Dr. Tobias.

"Your biblical comparison to this situation is apt but not quite correct," said Charles Cranwell. "The bad seed, in this case, left no evidence of its presence other than a mysterious sickness which has, so far, claimed a whole lot of lives. We don't even know what the seed is."

"The vehicle which sped away during the early morning hours—what can you tell me about it?" Tobias asked.

Mortimer Cranwell jumped in. "I heard it, myself. It could have been a pickup truck or four-by-four. I looked out the window but didn't see any lights—I could only hear it racing along the main road, through town."

"Could you pinpoint where the sound started?"

The sheriff gave the question some thought. "Not really. Only that it came from the east end and followed the main road."

"What's on the east end?" asked the doctor.

"There's a light industrial section and our water reservoir. The road starts up in the foothills where the mineral mine is located."

Tobias looked at his report. "There's no contamination in the water supply. We also can't find any correlation between the few light-industrial businesses, or the mine, in conjunction with the problem."

Tobias continued. "Several of the locals and tourists we've managed to interview think it's the presence of a UFO?" said Tobias. "Do you think there could be any extra-terrestrial cause to the event?"

Charles laughed. "Not a chance. That's all just baloney."

Tobias looked surprised. "Do you not believe in UFOs and aliens? Doesn't a part of your economy depend on the propagation of their presence in the area?"

"We use it for the development of a tourist industry for Hemlock, Dr. Tobias. My brother and I, however, have never seen anything which remotely suggests there is an alien presence. We have lived here all our lives and although there were times when we saw strange lights, I could never say that aliens were the source. There have always been rumors, but nothing concrete has ever been substantiated," said Charles.

"But your town benefits from it, does it not?"

"We all benefit but it's only for business purposes. People are curious and want to see for themselves—we supply the means for them to do so," said Mortimer.

"Do you think it may be possible for the military to have executed some sort of experiment which may have led to these deaths?"

"Your investigation should surely come up with something like that," said Charles. "We have no reason to think they would deliberately harm the town or its people."

Tobias set his report down on the desk. "I placed a call to the Surgeon General this morning to have Hemlock declared a state of emergency until we find the cause of the problem. I asked him to look into the Base's possible involvement—I don't have any jurisdiction with the military. He called me back a few minutes ago to say he spoke with the head of Edward's Air Force Base, of which Area 51 is an attachment. They deny that any of their personnel have been involved in a maneuver or operation close to Hemlock. They also deny there are classified experiments or trials anywhere close to the town."

The sheriff looked a little dubious. "We can't rule it out, though. Area 51 has always been opposed to our tourists going on hikes in the Groom Mountains. They say it could compromise their security. Several altercations between the military cammo-dudes and overzealous tourists have taken place in the past."

Charles jumped in. "I think it highly unlikely, bro. We have always been able to sort those matters out, and their cammo-dudes, although a bit rough, have never harmed anyone. If they are involved it would be a very difficult thing to prove."

"I have to return to Vegas—here's my card. If anything more happens please call me, any time of the day or night. I have arranged with the Surgeon General, who in turn has asked the military base's commander to keep a bus and a plane ready, should we need to evacuate the entire town. I am leaving two of my investigators here to sum things up and bring me back a final report by the end of the week—they will stay at one of the hotels. I will give my recommendations as to whether the town can continue to operate, after that."

Dr. Tobias and two of his colleagues left. They boarded the military bus and headed for the Base, where a transport plane waited to fly them back to Vegas.

\*

General Eugene Watkins scrutinized the report on his monitor screen and frowned. He knew of the incident at Hemlock. The event created little concern for him as Hemlock lay more than twenty-five miles, north of the base.

The general felt good about his offer of assistance to the stricken town. He felt glad to have helped them in their time of need and if anything, a sympathy for the Cranwell brothers, whose family business preceded the establishment of Area 51. The military could become quite obstinate with civilians, and Watkins imagined how the loss of Hemlock might affect the town's people and the Cranwell family business.

He glanced up at the framed picture of himself, which hung on the opposite wall. The silver stars looked good on his shoulders and he hoped to gain a promotion before he retired in the two years which still remained of his service. It would make a substantial difference to his pension. A knock on the door of his office jerked him out of his reverie.

"Come in," he said.

His personal secretary popped her head into the office. "Captain Benson is here to see you, General."

"Send him in, Enid."

She nodded and disappeared. A moment later Captain Ian Benson strode into the office and saluted.

"At ease, Benson. What's up?"

Benson, a large red-faced man, relaxed and removed his cap.

"Bad news, I'm afraid, Sir. You'd better come and see."

The general responded with a half-smile. "Something bothering you, Ian?"

"Ah...yes. It's the adjutant, Sir. We found him in Hanger 3."

The general jerked upright in his chair. "Hang-er 3? What on earth was he doing in there?"

"The adjutant is dead, Sir. We're not sure what he had discovered but as you know, he was not cleared for that area."

Watkins's face paled as he stood and almost knocked his chair over backward.

"Let's go. You can bring me up to date as we walk."

Ж

# 3

## Special Agent O'Malley

Deputy Director of the FBI, James Ingram, tightened his grip on the phone and stared out of the window as he waited for an answer from the recipient of his call. He knew his top field operative would put up an argument against an involvement in the case. Ingram could not blame his man, as Special Agent O'Malley and his family needed the rest, but their choice of Las Vegas as a holiday destination provided too good an opportunity for Ingram to pass up.

The silence on the other end told its own story. The deputy Director tried to reconstruct the facts in an attempt to make the requirement of O'Malley's involvement appear as a request, not a demand.

"You need to see this from the correct perspective, Dillon. You're the FBI's operative of the year and you are less than one hundred miles from Area 51. All I'm asking for is that you spend a few days, maybe a week with General Watkins, to find out what's going on."

O'Malley sighed in exasperation. "It's not me, Sir—it's Janet and Steven I'm thinking about. We've had little together-time this year and you know how complicated things are in my marriage."

Ingram pushed the envelope a little. "You've had a week together as a family. It's not as though we are trying to pull you away from them. All I ask is for a week—send Janet and Steve on a special excursion—the government will pay for it. Tell them it's in the interests of national security."

"Pardon me, Sir, but looking into one man's death and two missing scientists, is hardly in the national interest."

"It could quickly become so if we don't get a handle on this, Dillon. It's not just about the murder or the missing scientists—there is the question of the incident at Hemlock, the small town I told you about."

"I'll speak to Janet and call you back," said O'-Malley. His voice carried a certain skepticism but Ingram knew his man well. O'Malley instincts rivaled that of a true bloodhound. The mystery of Area 51 would draw O'Malley's curious mind and provide a golden opportunity to witness a few top secret operations.

"I'll give you one hour, O'Malley. This is very important to the White House and the Pentagon, so make sure you give it your full consideration."

"I will, Sir—you can bank on it," said O'Malley.

Mention of the White House meant more pressure for O'Malley to take on the case. He knew it would involve more than a few days of investigation, and Janet would not be pleased, but in the end, she would give in—she always did. Their marriage went through regular cycles of discontentment, which she blamed on her husband's specialized and dangerous work.

"Who was that, love?" asked Janet. She sat at the vanity with a brush in hand. The family looked forward to the evening's excursion at Caesar's Palace—the famous "Hoops on the Strip", arranged by O'Malley for his seventeen-year-old son, Steven.

He glanced pensively at her reflection in the vanity's mirror. "It was James Ingram, honey."

She turned and stared at him. "Is he bugging you about another case already?"

Janet always jumped right to the core. O'Malley nodded. "There's a problem out at Area 51 he wants me to have a quick look at since I'm so close."

"That man has no feeling for his subordinate's families," she said.

"He actually does care about us, Jan. He gave me all that time off after the last case if you re-member—told me to go heal my marriage—scolded me because I was in danger of losing you."

"Let's not talk about your ghastly affair with that Agostino woman," Janet stated.

O'Malley cast a dark look at his wife. "No—I agree, but the President has asked for me."

Her tone softened. "Little wonder, Dillon. You're their top special agent and also the FBI agent of the year, but it's a poor show when they can't give us a decent vacation."

O'Malley sounded a little more hopeful. "In-gram said the department would pay for any ex-cursion of your choice, here in Vegas, while I'm up at the Groom Lake Base."

"That sounds a bit like blackmail" Janet sug-gested.

"I guess you could say that. It makes a state-ment, though, regarding the need for my services as an agent. Ingram says it's in the interests of national security."

She gave him a dubious glance. "He always says that. He uses the President's name and the supposed interests of national security, to get your attention."

"I know, but it's hard for me to pass up such an opportunity to see Area 51—I've always wondered about that place. It would be like a special excursion as a part of my vacation."

Janet turned around in her chair to face him. "You know it won't just be a few days. These things have a habit of producing all sorts of complications and dangers—and you relish being in the midst of it, don't you?"

"I guess I do. It's my nature and you knew that when you married me."

"I never expected such a roller coaster ride, but you're right. Go phone your boss and be on your way. Steven and I'll pick the most expensive excursion we can find and get on with it."

O'Malley breathed a sigh of relief. "Thanks love. I'll call Ingram—he has probably already arranged passage for me from McCarran International."

Janet gave him a wry smile. "Make it as quick as you can. We'll try not to miss you, although Steve's going to be disappointed."

"I'll speak to Steve," said O'Malley. "Secretly I think he enjoys the fact that his dad has a dangerous job. Let's just go to the Palace and enjoy ourselves tonight."

*

O'Malley sat and gazed out of the window as the 737, dubbed as a "Janet Jet", took off and climbed into the early morning airspace, above the city of Las Vegas. The Janet transporters flew personnel to and from Area 51, from various points on the continent. In the seat next to him sat an attractive brunette, with striking green eyes and long, shapely legs, with a magazine in hand. Every now and then she would glance past O'Malley to see what could be seen through the window.

"Do this flight often?" he asked.

She flashed him a smile. "Three weeks now"

"It's my first time," answered O'Malley.

"Working in admin?" she asked.

"I guess you could say that," he said.

She nodded and returned to her magazine. The twenty-minute flight ended as the aircraft touched down on a single tarmac runway in the restricted zone of Area 51. Although still early in the morning the sun shone with an intensity in the azure sky, and a quick glance out of the window revealed the shimmer of heat waves on the desert's surface. A military bus awaited the thirty civilians who clambered off the aircraft. Everyone wanted to escape the desert heat and get to their air-conditioned offices. Most would return at 4:30 pm for the flight back to Vegas—all except those cleared to stay. Deputy Director James Ingram's arrangement for him to stay on the base included a dormitory room with an en-suite bathroom and a high-level clearance for access to top secret projects.

The bus dropped everyone off at the entrance to the base's main headquarters, where an aide waited on the steps. She held up a sign with his name on it, so O'Malley left the group and made his way toward her.

The aide smiled. "Mr. O'Malley?"

She gave his six-foot frame, wavy brown, hair and clean-cut features an appreciative glance. It seemed strange to be addressed as "mister." His normal designation of "special agent" carried a measure of authority, and to be addressed with the former title felt like a demotion, however, on this assignment, no one could know his real vocation. The Base Commander would be the only person to know O'Malley worked for the FBI. If anyone should ask, his business involved classified work. Given the nature of Area 51, the explanation would satisfy any such inquiry.

O'Malley nodded. "I am he," he said.

"Please follow me, sir. General Watkins is waiting for you."

They passed through the reception area and walked to the far end of the corridor where she turned a corner and entered a smaller reception area. O'Malley's medium sized duffle swung at his side while they waited for an older woman with gray hair to complete a phone conversation.

The Aide introduced O'Malley to the woman who appeared to be the General's secretary. She came out from behind the desk and beckoned him to follow. She stopped at a closed door and rapped twice.

"Bring him in, Enid," shouted the general.

O'Malley followed her into the office and set his bag down on the floor. Enid shut the door behind her as she left.

"Welcome Special Agent. Make yourself comfortable." he pointed to a chair.

General Watkins appeared to be a relaxed, easy-going person, but O'Malley detected a more complex and driven personality behind the pale, blue eyes.

"Did you enjoy the flight?"

"It was short," said O'Malley.

The general moved to the front of his desk and leaned against the desktop. He pulled a cloth from his pocket, removed his spectacles and started to clean them as he sized O'Malley up.

"Deputy Director Ingram speaks highly of you. I believe you're the one who brought Merlin Jones and his master computer down."

"Couldn't have done it without my team, General," said O'Malley.

"You on vacation in Vegas?"

"Yes, sir—along with my wife and son."

"My apologies to have cut that short for you, O'Malley, but we need someone to look into a problem here—I believe you've been briefed?"

"I have, but it would be good to hear your impressions."

"Good," said the general. "My adjutant was found dead in one of the hangers the day succeeding the first Hemlock incident—as you already know Hemlock's the small town about twenty-five miles north of here, in the foothills of the Groom Mountain range. They still mine some minerals there but other than that, Hemlock's a base for UFO sightings and sensation seekers. It attracts a huge number of idiotic alien and UFO researchers every year. They had people die from a stranger virus problem and a few days after that, two of my most valuable scientists went missing from the base."

"Can you tell me what those scientists were working on?" O'Malley asked.

"It's highly classified stuff, O'Malley. You'll have to sign a non-disclosure agreement with us. I'm not sure if the incidents are all connected but everyone here is quite shaken and some are in fear of their safety."

"Did these scientists leave the base at all—go for a walk or a hike?"

"The base is well protected and its unlikely anyone could get in or out without security knowing about it. We have searched the area thoroughly—there are not too many places where someone could be kept beyond their will, without drawing attention."

O'Malley inclined his head. "Is there a possibility of any project existing on the base you might not know about?"

The general shook his head. "It's highly unlikely."

"But not impossible?" asked O'Malley.

"No, I can't have my eyes everywhere and if someone wanted to pull something illegal they probably could, but I know the staff pretty well and I think such a scenario would be unlikely."

"I will need a quick rundown on all the operations currently being performed on the base and where they are. I'll also need your permission to ask certain questions of the staff."

The general returned to his chair and opened a desk drawer. "I anticipated your requirements and everything is on this flash drive. Highly classified work will only have a name and a designated area. You will be permitted into some of those areas, but only with a chaperone—do you have a laptop?"

O'Malley nodded. "I also have a revolver."

"Please make sure it's properly stored in the safe in your dorm room. I don't think you'll need it, but if you do, please keep it completely concealed on your person. I will expect some sort of a report from you by sundown, each evening."

"I'll do my best, sir."

The general leaned over the desk and extended his hand. "Enid will show you where the dorms are."

Ж

# 4

## The Groom Lake Base

The room surprised him. Small, but comfortable, with modern decor and an en-suite shower. The particular dorm accommodated military personnel above the rank of a captain and civilians, with high clearance designations. Enid assured him his high clearance appointment would give him a measure of notoriety with the general staff and earn him the respect of the personnel.

"You'll be taking meals in the general dining room—walk through those buildings over there and it's the gray building on your right, as you face the first airstrip. A member of the cleaning staff will be in on a daily basis to clean, and bed-linen will be done every second day. I'm sure your stay will be very comfortable, Mr. O'Malley."

He thanked her and she left. A window opened out onto a small patch of concrete on which a flag-pole stood. The Stars and Stripes fluttered in the slight breeze, and the slap of the lanyard beat a constant tattoo. The breeze would be a welcome respite from the heat of the day for those who worked outside or walked to their designated posts. O'Malley set out his clothing and toiletries, then sat down at the small desk provided. He opened his laptop and inserted the flash drive.

A schematic of the base's building layout popped up with a legend of building numbers and designations. He scrolled down to find all the various departments, each which provided the name of the lead supervisor plus a number for classified priority. There appeared to be three major, classified top secret projects on the go and at a guess, one or more of these could have been the focus of someone's intrusive interest; enough to involve a murder and abduction of senior personnel.

O'Malley's signature on the non-disclosure contract meant he could not breathe a word of the military's secret projects to any unauthorized or unconnected personnel. To do so could lead to imprisonment and the loss of his career. The flash drive would have to be returned and his laptop scrutinized, plus submission to a personal search, before his ultimate departure. It appeared the military took no chances with any of their contractors.

In order of classification, he made a mental note of the projects, their supervisors and department numbers. A brief description of each project provided him with some insight as to their depth of importance and he doubted whether anyone else on the base, other than the general and his adjutant, would have been privy to as much joint information. The list started with a nana-robotics project in a venue designated as Hangar-3. He opened a linked pdf file, which revealed the people involved. A name of interest appeared on this list —Dr. Roger Banning, one of the two missing scientists. A civilian scientist by the name of Robin Clandecker headed up the project.

The next project featured work on a hypersonic spy plane with an aeronautical engineer by the name of Alissa Cooper as the supervisor. He opened the linked file of names and read through the list. Two of the names duplicated from the first list. The third project focused on antigravity pulse engines and electromagnetic drives. He memorized all the details and tried to imprint the entire base layout on his mind. Two long runways, interconnected with shorter ones, gave the entire airfield an abnormal, oblong shape and adjacent to it, rows of hangars and service buildings. The dry, salt floor of the Groom Lake appeared white in the aerial photo, which showed its geographic position in the Nevada desert.

O'Malley glanced at his watch as a group of the general staff made their way below his window toward the dining hall. The growl of his stomach persuaded him to shut down the laptop and remove the flash drive. On the desk lay a pendant name tag and a plastic holder on a lanyard, which contained his personal details: "D. O'Malley, Base Logistics and Statistics."

He chuckled at the fictitious job description appointed him by General Watkins, as a cover. The tags lay on top of a typed description of his apparent duties, which involved base logistics and statistics. At the bottom of the tag were the letters, Q-RD, which gave him clearance to be involved with certain top secret projects and restricted data. Other people with this designation were the civilians and military personnel, who worked on the three classified projects.

O'Malley placed the flash drive into the small safe, situated in the room's closet. He keyed in a password as per the written instructions and tested it. Satisfied that his valuables would be safe he included his revolver and locked the door. He hung the lanyard around his neck, pinned the pendant tag onto the front pocket of his shirt and left.

*

Robin Clandecker leaned back in the chair like a desert cowboy on a runaway horse and motioned toward the entrance with his eyes. The man opposite him nodded as they spied O'Malley enter the dining facility and cross the floor, to the buffet counter.

"Is that him?" Clandecker asked.

"That's him," said Captain Benson.

"Do you think he's here to spy things out?"

"Not quite sure. The old man said we were getting a statistician from Washington DC who would help to do the adjutant's job while they looked for a replacement."

"Pity about Wally," said Clandecker.

"Yeah—it's a shame but he got too close. I kind of wish it had been someone else," answered Benson.

"Those other two morons also nearly messed things up. I guess they'll be replaced, as well."

"An unfortunate situation. We have to make sure all possible leaks are plugged."

Clandecker glanced at O'Malley, who with food plate in hand looked around at the half-filled tables for a place to sit. "Do we keep an eye on him?"

"He is the only new incumbent since Wally's death, so I would say it can't harm to be cautious."

\*

O'Malley looked around at the people who sat at the tables. A mixture of civilian contractors, staff members, and ranked military officers, sat in quiet conversation with each other. A few empty tables remained for him to sit alone which he would have preferred. However, the need to blend in, motivated him to join with someone and strike up a conversation.

He recognized the brunette from the Janet flight and sidled up to the table where she sat with her meal.

"Mind if I join you?"

"She looked up with the glimmer of a smile. "Sure, knock yourself out."

He moved a chair into position, sat opposite her and set his lunch down in front of him.

She sipped on a spoonful of soup, her eyes riveted on his face. "You sat next to me on the plane this morning," she said.

"Is that a condemnation or a confession?" he joked.

She chuckled and stuck out her hand. "Maria MacDonald."

"Dillon O'Malley." He took her hand and gave it a cursory shake. Her strong grip surprised him.

She squinted at the pendant tag on his shirt pocket. "A Q-RD, huh? You must be important."

He shrugged. "Not really. I'm here to check on the work statistics, and as an interim adjutant, while they find a replacement for Walter Greenberg."

"I see. Logistics and Statistics? It's a sad thing about Wally. I met with him on occasion with regard to some admin issues on occasion."

"Did you get to know him?" asked O'Malley.

"Not really. He appeared to be a nice bloke, very knowledgeable and good at his job."

O'Malley detected a faint twang to Maria's accent. "You from down South?"

"Originally from Florida—but I now live in D.C."

"Were you on holiday in Vegas?"

I decided to take a few days break and do some shopping," she said.

O'Malley scooped up a spoon full of pasta. "I come from New York, myself."

"Do you have family there?" she asked.

"My wife and son."

She gave him an appreciative glance. O'Malley often drew this type of appraisal from the opposite sex. The good looks, wavy brown hair and blue eyes inherited from his mother, wife of an Irish immigrant coal miner, presented a pleasant facade. O'Malley rarely smiled. He maintained an intense call-of-duty attitude, and while he appreciated a woman's beauty as most men do, he rarely allowed his mind to meander down the lane of frivolous indulgence or fantasy.

Maria MacDonald's green eyes flashed a hint of disappointment at his married status, but it passed quickly and she held his gaze for a brief moment, before looking down at her plate.

"Do you have just the one boy?" she asked.

"My wife and I had a daughter—Fallon. She died in a car accident on her prom night."

"That's an awful thing to happen," said Maria. "I am so sorry—you must miss her very much."

"More than words can say. How about you?" He wanted to change the subject.

"Just surfacing from a difficult divorce," she said.

"Sorry to hear that. How are you coping?"

"Every day gets better. I'm over it now, but it was hell for a while."

The woman attracted his interest. She came across as strong and independent, yet vulnerable. Short, dark hair, tanned skin, and a fine cheekbone structure gave her a regal look and the bright, green eyes gleamed like two emeralds in the artificial light.

He tore his eyes away from her face and focused on the plate of food in front of him. "When did you hear about Walter Greenberg's death?"

"About the same time as everyone else. It happened last week on Friday and the news spread quickly around the base. General Watkins said it appeared to be a suicide but no one is convinced and I doubt whether he believes it himself."

"What makes you think that?"

"People talk. It may be office gossip but they say his death happened under suspicious circumstances. A highly ranked officer whom I speak with at times said he thinks Wally paid the price for something he discovered."

"Did the officer say what he thought Wally might have discovered?"

"No, he didn't. Why all the questions, Mr. O'-Malley?"

He managed a weak smile. "Sorry, I didn't mean to pry. I was just interested to know what happened to him. After all, I have taken over some of his admin duties—please call me Dillon."

Maria nodded. "I guess everyone has questions about his death—and the disappearance of those other two scientists."

O'Malley looked up at the clock on an adjacent wall. "I guess lunchtime's over. I had better go to Wally's office and familiarize myself with some of the issues he was dealing with."

Maria raised manicured eyebrows. "Let me know if there's anything I can do to help. I assume you're staying on the base?"

He confirmed. "Are you?"

"In the civilian wing. If you find you have nothing to do in the evenings you can always catch a drink at Sam's Place—it's near the baseball field."

"Thanks, Maria. Maybe I'll see you there."

She nodded. "Bye, Dillon—look after yourself."

He left the mess and walked back to his quarters, where he pulled out his laptop and removed the flash drive from the safe. A quick check for Walter Greenberg's office showed him the exact locality.

*

Clandecker and Benson kept an eye on O'Malley as he sat down at Maria's table.

"Who's the broad?" Clandecker asked.

"Name's Maria MacDonald. She works in the material's coordination department. I wouldn't mind spending a night in her bed," answered Benson.

"You bet. It looks like our friend has cottoned onto her. How long has she been here?"

"About three weeks."

Clandecker looked thoughtfully at the couple. "About coincides with the second Hemlock incident."

"What're you thinking? Another spy, come to check up on things around here?"

"You never know—it's possible. I don't want to fall foul of a conspiracy theory, though."

"It won't hurt to keep an eye on them," said Clandecker.

Ж

# 5

## RC - UGH3

O'Malley found Greenberg's office without any problem. Typical of a military cubicle, a picture of Greenberg in an air force uniform, hung on the wall. On his desk stood a framed photo of his family. The Adjutant appeared to be in his late forties, married to an attractive blonde. The picture portrayed the couple with their young teenage daughter, all in a typical family pose. O'Malley locked the door, sat down at the desk and opened the top drawer, which revealed stationary items along with a notepad plus a clasp knife in a pouch, all placed in a neat order.

He opened the second drawer to find a book on military protocols, plus what looked like a journal, which he removed and placed on the desktop. The pages of the journal were arranged in the chronological order of the current calendar year, much like a diary, sectioned into months, weeks and days. O'Malley thumbed through pages of notes, made from the minutes of all the meetings attended by Greenberg that year, but no extraordinary events jumped out at him. He paged through the weeks of the current month, up to the day prior to Greenberg's death. His eye caught a scribbled entry at the bottom of the page, beneath figures which could have been the listing of daily fuel usage. It read:

*RC – UGH3? Doesn't make sense.*

O'Malley scrutinized at the entry. It appeared to be an afterthought and whether it related to the figures above, he couldn't be sure. He felt, however, it would be worth making a note of. He scribbled the sentence down onto a page from a desk pad and stored it in his wallet.

A filing cabinet stood in one corner, adjacent to a large safe. He replaced the journal, slipped out of the chair and opened the top drawer of the cabinet. Surprised that the drawers were not locked he thumbed through the file tags on each folder. They involved the base's statistics with regard to quantities of weapons, ordinance, vehicles and aircraft. A file which attracted his attention contained a list of all the personnel on the base; their names, designations and departmental appointments.

No personal records of individuals were present so he assumed the names served as Greenberg's staff contact information. There were at least seventeen hundred people on the base and any one of them could have been Greenberg's murderer.

O'Malley checked the other three drawers but found nothing of significance. Amongst some books stacked on the desktop beside the family photo, his eye caught sight of a Bible. Unfamiliar with the book he opened it out of curiosity and flipped through the pages. Halfway through, a piece of paper fell out and landed on the desktop. He picked it up and read the short paragraph which took up most of the sheet:

*RC and B records show discrepancies. Something not right. Where was all this time spent?*

He slipped the note into his pocket and replaced the Bible. Greenberg appeared to have found some records which didn't add up. What did, "RC and B refer records," refer to? Did the reference correlate with the journal scribble, which alluded to RC – UGH3? The letters "RC" were either a department or someone's initials. Reference to time spent, also raised a question—could it be work hours logged on a project?

It would not take O'Malley long to find out. He took one final look around the office, slid the deadbolt on the door back, and left. It came to mind that he saw Maria MacDonald's name listed under, "Department of Material Coordination" and he wondered what she did there. Much about her intrigued him. It could have been the strength of her handshake or the way she carried herself—some element of Maria's persona unsettled him. Since the short affair with Gabby Agostino, it became apparent that his marriage relationship no longer provided the fulfillment he longed for. His boss, James Ingram, had come to know of the affair and in an effort to save O'Malley from himself, offered the Agostino woman a promotion which provided her a posting to Jordan.

O'Malley's marriage problems started with the death of his sixteen-year-old daughter. A vehicle accident on her prom night snatched the girl from her family and created a huge rift between the parents. FBI counselors tried to help but the relationship seesawed between potential breakups and arguments, to short times of contentment. O'Malley blamed himself for his daughter's death. He lived each day with the knowledge that neither he nor the total compliment of the FBI was able to find the driver responsible for the accident.

His thoughts returned to Maria. She may not have told him the complete truth about herself, but did he really want to know? O'Malley did not think so, but an emotion deep within his sub-consciousness cried out for an intimacy his marriage no longer provided. When offered a promotion to the position of special agent, Gabby Agostino chose her career over a permanent relationship with him. In good conscience her decision reflected a resolve, to not be the cause of a marital breakup.

He understood and although disappointed he accepted the situation. Janet stuck by him when she should have grabbed her pride and dignity to get out of the relationship.

O'Malley decided to walk to the new headquarters building and speak to General Watkins's secretary, Enid. A pleasant woman in her fifties, Enid played the typical role of a military secretary. She ordered everyone around with a corporal flare and languished in her position of authority. Not immune to O'Malley's good looks she smiled at him when he appeared at her desk.

"What can I help you with, Mr. O'Malley?"

The title of mister still bugged him, but he took it as a necessary part of the mission.

"Who would be the best person to speak to with regard to the management of hours logged, on projects?"

"Each department has its own daily record of labor and the projects their hours to which they are logged. Which department would you like to see?"

"I'm not really sure. Do you have anything going on at UGH-3?" He didn't know what the "UGH" stood for but it had to be a known military acronym.

"UGH-3—or Hangar-3? I think it's used for storage, but you'll have to ask General Watkins."

"Any idea what they store there?" he asked.

"No idea at all, Mr. O'Malley—as I said, you need to talk to the General. Where did you come across the number UGH-3? It doesn't sound like an official number."

"Oh, just something I saw in Colonel Greenberg's journal. It's probably nothing."

O'Malley felt his gut lurch as Enid talked. Her answers seemed very quick off the tongue and a bit evasive. She most likely knew what UGH meant but because it might have a top-secret classification, she felt reluctant to talk about it.

"Is there a possibility of me talking with General Watkins?" he asked.

"Hang on, Mr. O'Malley. He's busy with the auditor at the moment. I'll find out when he'll be available."

She got on the intercom and after a quick word with the general reported back to O'Malley.

"Could you come back tomorrow at 5:00 pm?"

The General's office door opened and Maria MacDonald appeared. She saw him and her face lit up.

"Hi, Dillon. If you're looking for the General his busy with our internal auditor."

They walked down the corridor together and he could smell the faint scent of her perfume.

"Doing business with the general?" he asked.

Maria hesitated. "I needed to clear up something with regard to my appointment."

O'Malley sensed a guarded answer to his question. Could it be a possible attempt to hide the real reason?

"See you at dinner?" The question popped out of his mouth before he thought about the implications.

She raised her eyebrows and smiled. "Are you suggesting a date?"

He chuckled. "I am trying to get to know people."

"I guess that's a good enough reason. Dinner is at 6:00 p.m. I'll see you there."

Without another word, she headed for the building's exit.

*

Captain Benson, Conrad Kolke, and Robin Clandecker sat passively while they listened to the explanation. The words came in slow combinations of syllables and consonants, exacerbated by the equipment strapped over Maguilor's face. Drip tubes of saline solution, potent antibiotics combined with painkiller drugs, crossed over each other to every part of the emaciated body and the room looked more like a factory than a medical facility.

The question with regard to the intricacies of the electromagnetic drive caused Maguilor to search for a simpler interpretation of the concept.

Kolke shook his head. "I understand the concept of the electromagnetic drive. It has been around a long time, but you speak of warp bubbles forming within the closed system as the concept for interstellar travel. I don't see how these bubbles can form within the system."

Maguilor listened patiently to the reasoning. The translator, a contraption strapped over the lower half of his face, and linked to a computer, took milliseconds to find suitable words for the translation of his monolog. The digitalized sound of each word lacked the emotion his listeners would have liked, however, the information Maguilor shared, would always be priceless to them. With a sudden splutter of electrical static the linguistic converter died and brought their interview to an abrupt end. An electronic alarm sounded and within seconds a doctor accompanied by a medic, rushed in to check Maguilor's vital signs.

"You must leave now," said the doctor. His voice carried an air of authority as he set up a defibrillation process. Clandecker stood with his two colleagues and they cast disappointed glances at each other. Benson turned to the doctor as he stood to leave.

"Will we be able to speak to him again—perhaps tomorrow morning?"

The doctor looked doubtful. "I don't know. I'll contact you if it becomes possible."

Benson thanked him and they left the clinic.

Once outside the facility, they walked toward the main dormitory and mess area as the sun started its decline toward the horizon.

Clandecker addressed Kolke. "We're not far off making sense of this whole thing. Keep up the progress and our whole concept of space travel will be dramatically altered."

Benson chipped in. "Maguilor's knowledge has certainly made a difference to your project, Robin. Look what you've achieved with Omega. "

"It's the hours we're spending on trying to resolve the smaller issues, but the time has come for much bigger things." said Clandecker.

Benson agreed and then added a caveat. "Talking about the time spent on projects, I saw that new guy, O'Malley, slip into Greenberg's office and bolt the door. He's up to something and I think our suspicions about him may have some foundation."

Clandecker's eyes narrowed to slits. "Don't worry—he'll have to disappear like the others. I'll arrange it."

Ж

# 6

## An Interesting Correlation

Sheriff Mortimer Cranwell drove the school bus to the clinic. His heart wanted to fail him when he saw a lineup of people, outside the door and he wondered if the nightmare would ever end. Many of the town's people believed the catastrophe was the result of an alien presence and Mortimer did his best to convince everyone to remain calm. The news media speculated on a possible government conspiracy but the military flatly denied the allegations. Some journalists went so far as to say the Cranwell brothers were behind it all.

Mortimer stopped outside the clinic entrance and allowed people onto the bus. Some, helped by loved ones struggled to walk, and others appeared lethargic and slow. The Vegas Medical Commission's arrangement to set up a temporary field hospital on Hemlock's football field would diminish the time between onset and treatment. No one yet knew the underlying cause. Each case provided the forensic team with exactly the same symptoms and results. Not one of the victims survived. The mystery further deepened when not everyone in the town contracted the strange disease. Scientists attempted a process of elimination but without a satisfactory result.

The town's residents began to lose confidence in the medical authorities. Many closed their businesses and left the town to spend time with relatives in other parts of the country. The Cranwell brothers sent their family members away to relatives but vowed not to leave until answers could be found. They both continued to help the authorities with the investigation.

Sheriff Cranwell drove the bus onto the field and stopped at the entrance to the marquee. With the arrival of new life-support equipment, two more doctors and five nurses, the new facility boasted a high standard of technical capability. A total of thirty beds lined the sides of the large tent structure and a smaller tent served as a temporary morgue. The atmosphere remained somber and subdued as the doctors and nurses went about their duties.

Mortimer spent time with the patients, but some died before he could interview them. He gleaned as much from their families as he could and recorded each patient's daily habits and personal hygiene. The sheriff wondered when the ax would fall on his own family. Would the Cranwell brothers also succumb to the mysterious sickness?

Back at the office he set up a spreadsheet and began to fill in all the data. His questions included several not considered relevant by the medical team. One of these pertained to the use of bottled water, for drinking and personal hygiene. The result at the end of his summation drew one correlation: everyone who had contracted the virus drank water from the municipal supply. All those who remained unscathed drank bottled water.

This snippet of information posed a question: The municipal supply had been checked twice, and again that day. The tests came up clean. But, the question remained—why the correlation?

\*

O'Malley arrived at the dining hall a few minutes before 6:00 p.m. and found people lined up at the buffet counter. He did not see Maria, so he sat down at a table and waited. At six p.m. she walked in and stood in line to use the buffet. He joined her and they chatted while the lineup moved forward.

"I'm quite hungry. It's a problem living under these circumstances—have to spend a bit more time in the gym," she joked.

"You don't look like you need to lose any weight," he said.

"Thanks, Dillon, but I see myself in the mirror enough to know where I'm packing it on."

He allowed her to go ahead as they each took an empty plate.

O'Malley surveyed the bountiful spread. "What do you recommend?"

"The pastrami is always great, but it depends on what you like to eat," she said.

"I'm a carnivore. I love most meats, steak in particular."

"You won't be disappointed." She pointed to the rib-eye steaks. "I go mostly for salads or pasta. I find it sits better with me."

They dished up the items which took their fancy and then found an unoccupied table. Maria did not have a model's figure but he could see she worked out and took good care of herself. Her arms were firm, and her manicured hands elegant and strong. He thought she might have been an athlete in her younger years, perhaps a runner.

Maria looked up and caught his eye. "What?" she asked.

He blushed a little. "Nothing. I was just wondering if you were an athlete in your younger years."

"I did my fair share of athletics at school and university," she said.

"What did you do at university?" he asked.

"Trained in IT project management."

"Sounds complicated."

She put down her knife and took hold of the salt shaker. "How about you? With that top clearance designation, you must have specialized in something extraordinary."

"Not really. I trained in Quality Control," O'-Malley lied. He had prepared the answer in anticipation of her question. He didn't want her to become suspicious.

She sized him up. "I'm surprised. You have more of a military air about you."

"I spent time in Iraq—marines. Perhaps some of it never left me after final discharge."

"She looked dubious and changed the subject. "Did you hear about Hemlock?"

"The little town north of here? Sure, they've had some sort of virus problem."

Maria scowled. "It's more than a virus problem. Another whole group of people died today."

O'Malley absorbed the information and wondered if Greenberg's death and Hemlock and the two missing scientists, were not all part of the same problem.

"I heard Hemlock is one of those UFO towns. The military tried to shut them down in years gone by."

She leaned forward and lowered her voice. "Imagine if the military were trying to scare the town people off. I wouldn't put it past them."

O'Malley frowned. "It would seem an extreme measure."

"Imagine if Greenberg's death and the two missing scientists are a part of it."

He almost choked. These had been his very thoughts.

"You're doing a lot of imagining," he said.

She smiled and downed the last of her pastrami. "I know. Don't mind me—I'm a bit of a romantic."

O'Malley laughed and finished off his steak. "Going for dessert?"

"Of course, can I get you some?" she asked.

"Thanks. I'll have some trifle."

After dessert O'Malley brought coffee and they continued with small talk. At 7:10 p.m. Maria leaned back in her chair. "I know it's only your first day, but have you seen much of the base?"

"Only what lies between the Main admin and the dormitories."

"Would you like the short tour?" she asked.

To spend more time with her sounded appealing. "Sure. Why not."

They left the facility and walked outside into the cool night air. Adjacent to the hall stood the Administration and supply buildings.

"This is where I work," said Maria. She pointed to her office window.

"You do material coordination? Isn't that a bit below your education level?" asked O'Malley.

"I'm in charge of all materials on the base, among other things. My main job is to ensure that the material specifications are correct. I'm also in charge of data input."

O'Malley countered. "Sorry, I didn't mean my question to be disparaging."

"Not at all. You're welcome to your opinion. Most people don't have a clue what the job title conveys—it's a bit misleading."

The lights of the base illuminated the runways, which spread out in different directions before them. O'Malley could see the extent of the operational area as they breasted the building perimeter and walked toward the service road, which connected to the first runway.

"That's the old runway, no longer in use. It was built in the early sixties," she said. "Further, over there in the distance is the main runway which is in daily use."

O'Malley looked around in wonder and pointed to a structure, between the service road and the old runway. "—and that's the control tower over there?"

"Correct. They're quite busy with all the Janet jets leaving, and arriving, from various parts of the country."

"I believe the security is extremely tight."

Maria nodded. "Tighter than Fort Knox. There are devices set along the perimeter that can tell the difference between a human and an animal. The guys who patrol the area are called cammo-dudes, because of their uniforms—they're not military, but contractors."

"You know a lot about this place, Maria. I've always wanted to come to Dreamland and test out the alien theories."

Maria chuckled. "Do you believe there's life out there—in outer space, I mean?"

"I'm a bit of a skeptic but I guess it's possible. I hold agnostic views about these things."

"I've been a believer since I was a little girl, hence my interest in Area 51." she said.

They stepped onto the service road and walked south toward the Janet Terminal. Maria turned up the collar of her windbreaker to protect against the cool evening breeze. Their elbows touched on occasion as they sauntered along the road, their focus on all the satellite dishes and variety of teleme-try equipment. Above them, millions of stars twin-kled as the heavens reached down to join with the Earth on the distant horizon.

The sound of a vehicle behind them caused Maria to glance over her shoulder. They thought it would pass by but it stopped next to them. Two cammo-dudes jumped out and approached. O'-Malley thought it might be a check of credentials and stood his ground, but Maria, tensed up and took a step back.

"What's going on?" asked O'Malley.

"We have orders to take you to our supervisor, sir." The man who spoke stood at least six foot, five inches tall and his tone did not sound friendly.

"On what grounds," queried Maria.

The second man, shorter than his colleague, jutted out his chin. "You are in a restricted area."

"You're joking, surely," snorted O'Malley. The tall dude pulled out a set of handcuffs.

"Put out your hands please."

His colleague did the same to Maria and before they knew it the two men shoved them into the back of the vehicle.

"You can't do this to us. No special clearance is required to be on the service road," Maria complained.

"We're simply following our orders," said the tall dude.

"There has to be some mistake. I have a Q-RD clearance and I'm permitted to be anywhere on the base at any time," said O'Malley.

"You can sort it out with our boss—now if you don't mind, I have a headache," said the second dude. The original politeness had vanished.

The four-by-four roared off down the service road in the direction of the security building. O'-Malley's gut told him the encounter spelled trouble for him and Maria. Could someone have blown his cover? Were these the people who murdered Greenberg and abducted the two scientists?

# 7

## The Base Security

The men parked their vehicle behind the offices, at the back entrance. O'Malley looked around for anyone who might be in transit to the dorm area but saw no one. The two cammo-dudes bundled their victims into the Security building and along a passageway to a dark room, which appeared to be a cell.

One of the men switched on a dingy light, the product of a single lightbulb in the ceiling and proceeded to release the handcuffs.

"Make yourselves comfortable," said the large cammo-dude. A gate clanged shut and they turned to stare in astonishment at each other. A single bench ran across the length of the room, against the back wall. Little option remained but to sit down and wait. The outside wall contained no windows and the cell smelt dank due to an apparent lack of air-conditioning.

"Well, this is a surprise," said O'Malley.

Maria did not seem too perturbed. "I'm sure it's just a mistake. They said their supervisor would be along to speak to us and once he finds out who they have arrested, those two assholes will get their butts kicked."

O'Malley didn't share Maria's enthusiasm and he suspected his cover had been blown. It spawned an anxiety—that her life might be in danger because of him. She sat next to him with arms wrapped around her torso, and in an effort to warm up, kept the collar of her windbreaker turned up. They had no option but to wait for the supervisor.

"They didn't even search us," said O'Malley.

"No need—no one is allowed to carry weapons within the base perimeter unless authorized. Those cammo's may have possessed cuffs, but they weren't carrying any weapons."

O'Malley thought of his glock, which lay in the dorm room's safe. It would have been a great comfort to have it on him. He had not expected problems so early in the game but it seemed obvious his appointment must have attracted some unwanted attention. The tall cammo-dude reappeared, unlocked the cell door and motioned to O'Malley. "Boss wants to talk to you."

"Thank God. Now we can get this fiasco sorted out." He turned to Maria. "I'll be back, don't go anywhere."

She gave him a weak smile and said, "I won't."

O'Malley followed the tall dude down the passageway to the front area, into a small office, where a man sat behind a desk staring at a computer monitor. The other cammo-dude pulled up a chair for O'Malley and took up a position behind him.

O'Malley sat down and composed himself. The man opposite him, who had to be the security supervisor, seemed unapologetic. He wore a smirk across his pock-marked face and the broad nose with heavy eyebrows completed the facade. He eyed O'Malley with intent and leaned back in his chair.

"So, our great and illustrious FBI agent thought he could hide his identity," said the supervisor.

The words shook O'Malley to the core. Ingram had not thought it necessary to give him an alias— not that it would have mattered. Someone must have tipped the security off as to his real purpose at Area 51.

"What's the meaning of this?" asked O'Malley.

"The meaning is very simple, O'Malley—you've been sent to spy on base activities and we do not take kindly to that."

"I'm here for the base's good. Who tipped you off? My appointment was made at the highest level and if you know what's good for you..."

The supervisor interrupted. "We do know exactly what's good for us, Special Agent. We were tipped off by someone at a high level. We don't need you sneaking around the base because we are quite capable of doing that ourselves."

O'Malley couldn't help a smirk. "A man has been murdered and two scientists have disappeared. What have you discovered so far?"

"We don't need to discover anything, O'Malley. We know what happened to these people. They meddled in business that didn't concern them."

A chill went down O'Malley's spine. "Are you saying you know what's going on?"

The man's tone changed. "This is something much bigger than the both of us and we can't have you meddling in it."

"What about Miss MacDonald?" O'Malley ventured.

It's a pity you drew her into this, but I'll let her go. She's just a civilian and can't do any harm to our cause, but you, on the other hand—"

O'Malley's gut signaled danger. "You don't intend to let me go, do you? You're the one who murdered Greenberg and probably those two scientists, as well."

The supervisor remained silent but maintained the smirk on his face.

"You must know the FBI will come looking for me. They will use all their resources and they will find you."

"Nobody will be able to prove a thing, O'Malley. They'll certainly find us but they will never find you. We won't deny we took you into custody but the story will be that you returned to Vegas, and no one has seen you since."

O'Malley fumed but kept a facade of calm. Maria didn't know his real identity, but she would be sure to go to General Watkins and a search would be initiated. The thought of Maria going to Watkins bothered him. What if the general turned out to be involved? Who at a high level, had tipped off the enemy?

He heard a movement behind him and turned his head but the blow caught him unawares.

*

Maria waited for at least an hour before she began to experience pangs of fear for O'Malley. When one of the dudes appeared he closed the door to the cell area so she had no view of the corridor. The sound of a heavy object being dragged past the cell, with an occasional grunt and curse, alerted her. The noise disappeared, through the back door and she heard the four-by-four pull away. Moments later the door opened and the supervisor appeared.

"I am sorry to have kept you, Miss MacDonald," he said.

"How did you know my name?" she asked.

"Mr. O'Malley told us who you were and I apologize you had to be drawn into this but he is an imposter and we needed to apprehend him before he caused some confusion at the base."

Maria looked shocked. "What harm could he possibly do? I found him to be quite charming."

"I'm sorry I can't discuss this with you. If you have any complaints you can address them to the base commander."

"I certainly will speak to General Watkins. Your men were quite rude and rough."

"I do apologize if you felt badly treated, Miss MacDonald, but the men were just doing their duty. They are contractors who patrol the base and perimeter at night."

"What are you going to do with Mr. O'Malley?"

"We will continue to hold him until he is formally charged. He is kicking up quite a fuss."

"I'm sure he is," she said.

"Anyway, I will escort you back to your dormitory, or over to Sam's Place, if that's where you want to go," said the supervisor.

He had not introduced himself. "There is no need for that, Mister...." Maria started.

"Lieutenant Richard Blake," he responded. "You're free to go, Miss MacDonald."

She gave him a frosty stare and pushed past him, to leave.

"Remember, if you have any problems about this evening feel free to contact the general." his voice, filled with condescension, floated after her.

The front area appeared empty and she assumed they had taken O'Malley to another location. Outside in the cool night air, Maria jogged to the corner of the security building and then west, to the dormitories. She needed to find out where they had taken O'Malley. The entire event reeked of conspiracy and she suspected Lieutenant Blake, along with his cammo-dudes, were involved. At long last, a positive lead had presented itself.

Maria clambered up the steps of the dormitory and ran down the corridor to her room, flung open the door and went straight to the closet. It took a few seconds to key in the password to the safe. She pulled out the .38 snub-nosed revolver, unzipped her windbreaker and strapped on a shoulder holster. With the gun secured under her arm, she pulled the windbreaker back on, hurried out of the room to the exit, and into the night. The three-week stay at the Dreamland Resort had given her an intimate knowledge of the base. Although Maria MacDonald's appointment had come via the normal civilian recruitment contractor in Vegas, her real name was Tammy Clyde-Walker.

*

O'Malley woke up a few minutes later with his hands and feet cuffed. His head hurt and he felt the wet, stickiness of blood, down the back of his neck. The cammo-dude must have struck him with the butt of a rifle. Starlight filtered through the darkened window of the vehicle. He could hear the sound of the tires on the service road with its typical vibration over the concrete surface. He wondered where they were taking him. A moment later the vehicle pulled to a stop and he heard the hum of an electric overhead gate. The vehicle pulled off again and the starlight changed into orange, candescent lights, mounted high up on the sides of concrete walls. They appeared to be in an underground bunker. The vehicle braked, turned and came to a stop. Seconds later the hatch door of the four-by-four opened and strong hands grabbed his fettered feet. Two men hauled him out, to dump his body on the hard concrete floor. He pretended to be out for the count.

"Get him into the storeroom." The voice of the tall cammo-dude filtered through to his groggy mind.

Hands gripped O'Malley's wrists and dragged his inert body to a small storeroom, where the cammo-dudes left him.

"Make sure he stays quiet until tomorrow morning," shouted the tall dude.

"Not that anyone will hear him down here," answered his colleague.

By the short conversation, O'Malley discerned he had several hours to find a way out of his predicament. Small mercies, he thought. He had to be in a secret, underground facility of some kind. The walls around him were concrete and dank.

*

Tam Clyde-Walker sprinted between the buildings in the direction taken by the four-by-four. The sound of the tires on the concrete and the roar of the motor, confirmed a destination further south. She would have to hurry to catch sight of the vehicle's return, once the cammo-dudes had deposited their human cargo. Tam scurried past hangar eighteen toward the southern taxiway and stopped at the corner of hangar twenty, for a quick breather. Minutes later the four-by-four rose up out of the depths of the Earth, from an underground facility beneath Hangar-3. Walter Greenberg had referred to it as UGH-3. No one knew any details about the facility's purpose—no one would talk about it. She would need to find a way in.

# 8

## Exploring the Correlation

Mortimer Cranwell leaned back in his chair and stared at the spreadsheet. The correlation in the data intrigued him. Hemlock's water supply versus the use of bottled water for drinking purposes did not figure in any of the investigator's reports. He concluded the reason for this to have been the strict tests applied to the municipal supply. Beyond a small residue of foreign matter, the water had proved drinkable. The town filtration drew water from a large subterranean lake, pumped up through a borehole at the base of the mountains and stored in a concrete reservoir, situated at the outskirts of Hemlock.

The evidence seemed coincidental but the more Cranwell thought about it the more he felt it could be an issue. He picked up the phone and placed a call to Dr. Tobias, the head investigation scientist.

"Dr. Tobias? I think I may have found something."

He explained the correlation and Tobias listened with patience. "It seems unlikely but we'll look into it."

"What if the poison or the virus, whatever it is, dissolves after a certain time?"

The scientist sounded skeptical. "I don't know how possible it would be to hide the evidence so completely even after a long while, let alone such a short duration, but we can't rule anything out. I will have them test the water again."

'Thanks, Doc. Let me know when it's done."

"I will. We're getting a little desperate to find a cause—the twenty-third victim has just died."

"I must say I'm getting a little nervous about the rumors of an alien presence. Some of the locals are saying it must have something to do with Area 51, but I am a little ambivalent with regard to an alien invasion."

"Is that the theory?" Tobias asked.

"Its spread like a wildfire and now we have people from all over the world trying to make bookings at the hotels. They're not even put off by the fact people are dying."

"It's a nutty world, Sheriff," answered Tobias.

"This entire saga is totally nuts. I am going to petition the military to place a watch on Dreamland's activities. If some type of advanced experiment is being performed by the military, the government should know about it."

"Perhaps the government does know about it, however, as I said before—we can't rule anything out."

Dr. Tobias ended the conversation and Cranwell continued to stare at the computer screen for a while. After some reflection, he moved over to the coffeemaker to set up a brew. It struck him as odd that Charles made a recent decision to change the consumption of municipal water at their town office, in favor of the bottled variety. His brother maintained the hard subterranean water contained traces of shale which damaged the filters after a while and scaled up the pipes with calcium. Not long after that Mortimer followed suit at the law office. Charles, the studious one in the family, led the way as he always did. His law degree, supplemented with a Master's in Economics meant he could have landed a job with some huge financial company and climbed its corporate ladder. A love for the family business, however, combined with the concept of Hemlock, attracted Charles's sense of entrepreneurship.

Mortimer, on the other hand, lived in his brother's shadow. He followed along with whatever Charles proposed. But for Charles's insistence, his younger brother would have been content with the oversight of the mine and its mineral production. A short course at the police academy in Vegas paved the way for the appointment as Hemlock's first sheriff.

With the current problem they faced, he felt quite overwhelmed and responsible to produce a result in the overall investigation.

He thought about the water supply and the correlation. If the municipal water turned out to be a factor, then Charles would have saved their lives. Due to the hard water problem in Hemlock, Charles's investment in a small Vegas company that bottled water paved the way for the best wholesale prices for the town's only supermarket. Mortimer's wife never drank from the local water supply and encouraged the family to be more conscious of a filtered water intake on a daily basis. He would not have bothered, and but for her encouragement, his family might have continued to drink the local water.

If it did factor into the equation he would be forever grateful to her and Charles, for their insistence on good diets and clean body hydration.

*

O'Malley turned over onto his back and wriggled into a position where he could lean against the wall.

The room appeared to be used for storage of janitorial and medical supplies. A crate labeled, "Medical Gloves" and another "Cleaning detergent," appeared to make up the bulk of the storeroom's inventory. He thought it odd that medical supplies would be stored in an underground facility. He looked up at the storeroom's door and saw a stenciled designation number: "Hangar-3. Supplies."

It took a moment before the truth hit him. *Hangar-3 Underground bunker. UGH-3.*

The notation in Greenberg's journal—it had to stand for, "Underground Hangar number three.'"

He made an effort to clear the grogginess from his mind and recall the full notation made by the adjutant, before his death: *"RC – UGH-3? Doesn't make sense."*

It made sudden sense to O'Malley. RC might be someone's initials or a department's acronym. The point came across with clarity. Hanger-3's project posed the strongest possibility of a connection to the adjutant's death and whatever Area 51 hid from the world. He reflected on his predicament. Now that these people knew his real identity they would dispose of him. Maria would go to General Watkins and complain about the cammo-dudes and their supervisor. If the base commander had no involvement, O'Malley might be rescued but thought of the alternative spawned by the general's complicity, only served to paralyze him with fear.

He needed to find a way out. The first order of the process required him to get his hands under his rump and work them toward his feet. With his knees bent and arms stretched to their limits, he managed to slip his cuffed hands under his feet. FBI agents went through hours of rigorous training to prepare them for such scenarios. The cuffs chafed his wrists until they almost bled, but the maneuver worked. He removed a straight wire-insert from his belt and went to work on the cuffs. In the early years the purpose for such training seemed like a waste of time, but in the moment, O'Malley thanked the trainers for their foresight.

A few moments of wiggle and jiggle with the wire sprung the lock of the wrist cuffs and after that, the ankles. He stood up to facilitate the flow of blood through his body.

O'Malley glanced at his watch: 8:30 p.m.

*

Tam waited for the four-by-four to pass on its way back to the security building before she broke cover and ran down the service road, to the south taxiway. Well hidden from view, the bunker entrance on approach to the hangar structure, could not be seen at ground level until an observer stood at the top of the ramp, and looked down at the security gate entrance. There were no signs to advertise the bunker's presence—as a top secret facility it took its designation from Hangar-3, a structure which served as a warehouse.

Tam thought the underground facility might be a "scoot and hide" structure, designed to get aircraft off the runway before they could be observed from above. The concrete ramp declined for twenty yards, up to the entrance gate. There would be no way through the gate and her mind raced to remember the briefing received prior to her mission; how to enter underground facilities through the air vent shafts, which in military applications, should be big enough to accommodate a human body.

She looked across the area of ground, which stretched over the top of the facility on the east side of the hangar and spotted several ventilators, spaced at various intervals. The standard CIA multi-tool issue, hooked to her belt, would prove useful in the event of internal wire mesh barriers. Without hesitation, she ran to the ventilator and gave it a quick inspection. Eight, 12 mm construction-issue bolts, held the top of the vent to the pipe. It took a few minutes to remove them, free the vent-top and place it on the ground. The pipe appeared large enough for her to slide into, and her runner's soles took decent purchase on the sidewalls as she maneuvered herself downward in the dark. A junction at about ten feet, allowed a horizontal investigation but she knew the further down the duct reached, the more exclusive the area would be.

The section dropped another ten feet and then bottomed out to provide a junction to the right. The bunker appeared to have two floors. She followed the horizontal and reached a junction off to the left. Light began to filter through the darkness from its further end and Tam realized it led to an outlet. After a crawl of eight more feet, the pipe ended at the bunker's outside wall. The diameter of the pipe became smaller, enough that it became necessary to wriggle and force her body through. She reached the outlet, a metallic, gauze cover, which appeared to be bolted to the inside bunker wall.

Tam lay still for a few moments, in the semi-darkness and tried to figure out how to overcome the obstacle. The interior of the bunker room, into which the outlet opened, became more visible as she pressed her face up against the outlet's wire-mesh cover. A hospital-style bed and a myriad of drip lines festooned the immediate area; equipment and medical apparatus lined the wall beyond the bed. The bed held a figure. The odd shaped head, with a contraption strapped to the lower face, made it difficult for her to make it out. No one else appeared to be in the immediate vicinity and she went to work on the bottom corner of the thick, gauze cover.

It took ten minutes to cut along the bottom of the gauze and halfway up the sides, which allowed it to be folded outwards like a flap and allow her body enough room to squeeze by. She wriggled through the gap and dropped the six feet to the floor. A quick glance in all directions confirmed the area to be a medical facility.

Tam crept forward to have a look at the patient. On arrival at the foot of the bed, her jaw dropped and she clapped her hand over her mouth, in an effort to stifle a scream.

# 9

## The General and his Goon

Lieutenant Richard Blake sat deadpan opposite General Watkins. His pock-marked face showed no signs of emotion as the general tore a strip off him. Beside a flare of the nostrils, an observer would have said he looked bored, however, tiny droplets of perspiration popped out on his brow to glisten under the rays of the overhead, neon lights.

"Why on god's earth did you allow those contractors to take the two of them together? Now I'll have to deal with her questions and make up a good story for having them apprehended."

"I apologize for the men, Sir. I told them to bring O'Malley in, not thinking he would be out taking a romantic, moonlight stroll with a woman. The fact he was not alone failed to faze them, unfortunately—they're really just mercenaries. O'-Malley is presently cuffed and locked in a storage room on level one."

Watkins did not look pleased. "We have to keep a lid on this thing. Questions will come from the deputy director when O'Malley disappears. I had to agree to his appointment after Greenberg's demise and the two scientists went missing. Now we have a witness that our own security took him by force—I don't want to attract any more attention to the base."

"Shit happens. We have Captain Benson to thank for that—his cover-up was too flimsy. What do you want me to write in my report, Sir?"

"You'll need to concoct a story about O'Malley breaking some rule and then being questioned for it. I'll arrange for it to appear he decided to catch the early morning's Janet flight to Vegas after you've released him. I'll find someone to stand in for him on the flight. The Vegas airport authorities will record his disembarkation on the other side and it will be off our hands from there. I'll also deal with this MacDonald woman, but she too may have to be eliminated, if necessary."

"We're taking O'Malley to Hemlock in the morning. I've made arrangements for him to follow in the footsteps of the two scientists—nobody will ever find him. Things should quieten down after that," said Blake.

"I certainly hope so, Lieutenant. O'Malley has only been here for one day and already he suspects the legitimacy of the project in Hangar-3."

Blake stood and gave a short salute. "I'll set up a charge sheet for O'Malley, Sir. It will show we wanted to question him on a possible violation of carrying a cell phone into a restricted top secret area, and that we later released him to his own devices."

*

O'Malley exited the storeroom and surveyed his surroundings. To the left, a tunnel extended into the rest of the bunker's first level, and on the right, he could see the main entrance gate, which led outside. An office with what appeared to be a lunchroom built into the wall of the cavern on the perimeter of the vehicle park provided an area for admin and personnel. The standard, orange candescent lights lit up the entire internal area. The tunnel extended on toward destinations unknown to him. The orange light shone an eerie glow throughout the immediate area and cast shadows from the two parked vehicles.

He crept past the SUV and four-by-four to peep through the office window—a desk with a computer, phone, and a filing cabinet, caught his attention. The entire area appeared to be unoccupied for the moment, and he assumed the few personnel were either between shifts, or elsewhere occupied. The unlocked office door extended an invitation to check the contents of the desk drawers where, after a short search, he discovered a set of keys for the cabinet.

Except for a few items the drawers were empty. O'Malley left the desk and turned his attention to the cabinet with the hope of more important discoveries. The top cabinet drawer, labeled "H-3 Bunker Purchases and Inventory," contained several files with stationery purchases and inventory, office equipment and expenditure on vehicle services. The second drawer's files reflected hours allocated to work performed within Hangar-3 and its bunker. With ears tuned for the approach of staff members, he scanned the pages of labor allocations. His memory returned to Greenberg's journal, with regard to the comment on the notation of RC and B: "Something is wrong," and "where was all this time spent?"

He discovered that the letters "RC" referred to the name on the corresponding labor log—R. Clandecker; head scientist, and the letter 'B' corresponded to Captain Ian Benson. The hours logged to one particular classified project, amounted to more than three thousand. Greenberg's body, found in a restricted area not named in the official report, pointed to the possibility of Hangar 3. These records must have been what Greenberg referred to in his journal. It would appear that perhaps someone discovered the adjutant in this very office, busy with the same records.

He replaced the file and fingered through several others. A file marked RE-Ac 1 caught his attention. He removed it from the cabinet drawer, sat down at the desk and began to look through the contents.

The project's initial report started with a news article from a Phoenix newspaper, in March 1997:

*"Strange Lights over Phoenix spark's claims of UFO's presence."*

O'Malley read on through the report of the encounter and he remembered the incident in the News, from his college years. A corresponding article covered the disappearance of four young men, the bodies of whom were never found. The blowup of a photo, taken at night, showed the remains of a craft shrouded in smoke, amongst the rocks and bushes of the Arizona desert. He did not recall it in a newspaper or any other journal on UFOs. The size of the craft appeared too big to be the remains of a crashed F-15 fighter jet, as claimed by the military.

He recalled from old news reports that the air force mobilized a squadron of F-15's that night and one crashed due to unknown causes, but enthusiasts claimed the military shot down a UFO. The military also said the strange lights over Phoenix were the results of flares dropped for the purposes of the training exercise. Pictures of the lights continued to cause controversy to the present day. What appeared more important to O'Malley were the letters, Ac 1, scribbled in pen, at the bottom corner of the photo.

His imagination raged through possible solutions for the letters, 'Ac'. Two words came to him; words that stuck and seemed to make sense—Alien Craft. His beliefs in alien invasion theory were zero until that point, but as he stared at the photo his doubt began to waiver. What if the air force had encountered an alien craft that night in 1997, and shot it down? What would they have done with the wreck and where would be the best venue to hide and inspect it? Area 51 would be the ideal place.

He replaced the file and continued his search. Seconds later he pulled out another file with the designated heading: "Omega". He opened it and picked up a document. The letterhead read, "E.M. Technologies", and it referred to a delivery for military use. It confirmed the sale of four drums, which contained a solution called "nano-organic catalyst". O'Malley frowned at the description and then shoved the letter back into the file. A noise caused him to stop and listen for a moment. The steel security gate had started to open, which meant the entry of a military vehicle with bunker personnel, and he needed to leave.

O'Malley slipped out of the office and jumped into the back of the closest vehicle, a four-by-four similar to the one the cammo-dudes used. He lay down on the backseat and elevated his head, just enough to see out of the darkened window, as the vehicle entered the bunker. A four-by-four appeared and parked adjacent to the one in which he hid. Two people got out. He did not recognize the voices but could hear the conversation as they stood beside their vehicle.

*

Captain Benson and Robin Clandecker drove down the ramp and waited for the electric security gate to open, then entered the bunker, beneath Hangar-3. Benson parked the vehicle in level one's parking area, outside the office and they both got out. Two other vehicles stood beside theirs.

"So we have him in custody?" asked Clandecker.

Benson slammed the vehicle's door closed. "In the storeroom. He'll be taken off the base in the morning—to George's Pit."

Clandecker closed the passenger side door. "What did the old man say?"

"Said he would deal with the girl if she gave any problems."

"The MacDonald woman? I know her. Let's hope she doesn't cause shit. Enough people have had to be disposed of," said Clandecker. "What time are you going to move Mr. FBI?"

"I told the old man it would be first thing in the morning," answered Benson.

"Good. It'll be great to get things back on an even keel again."

"Are we going to do any more runs to Hemlock? The tests seem quite conclusive, so far."

"I think we're pushing our luck if we continue, Ian. Besides, I don't like being the cause of so much misery. Both generals are happy that we've achieved the results for the launch of Omega. "

"Have to go. I'll see you in the morning, said Clandecker."

*

Tam could not believe her eyes. The creature on the bed did not look like a human. The odd-shaped head bulged at the temples and the large, slanted eyes, at least six inches apart, remained closed. The face below the temples narrowed down to a chin which curled upward to a point. The skin appeared to be more like an alligator's than human and the top of its head sprouted tufts of shoulder-length hair, which hung down each side. The elongated torso dominated her first impression and there did not appear to be genitalia. Two large feet, each with sharp goat-like hooves, stuck over the end of the bed and she judged the creature to be over seven feet in height. An instrument, strapped below the eyes hid what might have been a nose and mouth, from view.

She stood rooted to the spot and stared in hor-ror. Before she could regain composure the beast's one eye flicked opened and it stared back at her. The words came with a slow deliberation, combined with clicks and static, as though the creature spoke through an electronic device. A small light on the bridge of the equipment flashed green and red as the monster took in slow, deep breaths.

"Who...are...you?" She nearly fainted and it took a few moments to regain composure.

"My name is Maria. She decided to go with her alias despite the fact that soon her cover would be blown

"M...aria?" The words came quicker than his first sentence. "I am...Maguilor."

Her fright now began to dissipate as training kicked in.

"Who are you, Maguilor?"

"I am the commander of the Stellar Throne. The ship you call Ac-1."

"Where is the Stellar Throne now?" she asked.

"It was shot down by your military—many of your earth years ago. I am told the wreckage lies on the floor, above level one—in Hangar-3...."

The creature began to cough and splutter. An alarm went off on the vital signs monitor and Tam knew she would have to leave. The sound of foot-steps, on the run, came from further down the tunnel.

"Please don't tell them I was here, Maguilor."

His eyes blinked. Tam hoped the reaction came in recognition of her request. She swung herself up into the vent and squeezed back through the sev-ered gauze cover, into the vent pipe. The sound of footsteps entered the clinic and she hoped the compromised vent cover would not be discovered until she found O'Malley and escaped from the bunker.

# 10

## More About that Correlation

Mortimer Cranwell snatched his phone off the desk. "Sheriff's Office."

Dr. Tobias's calm voice sounded in his ear.

"Sheriff? I've had our lab recheck the water from Hemlock's main supply and we've had another look at the tiny residue which they picked up on the original tests. We have no reason to believe the residue stems from anything other than a natural source."

"How can you be sure?" replied Cranwell.

"We can't be sure at this stage but the residue has to be the result of a phenomenon which occurs under natural circumstances in the subterranean catchment.

"So, you're saying our water supply is okay and we should continue using it? What about the correlation?"

Tobias hesitated. "I would say the water is safe. The fact that all the unaffected people used bottled water is a poignant factor, but we can't find anything poisonous in Hemlock's water supply to make it conclusive—it's your call, though."

"I think we'll keep things as they are at the moment. I'll arrange with my brother to truck water in from our nearest neighbor. We have two auxiliary storage tanks which can be used in the interim. The regular water supply will be cut off until further notice."

"I'm sure we'll soon get to the bottom of it," said Tobias.

Mortimer ended the conversation and placed a call to his brother. Charles sounded a bit dubious. "Are you sure you want to do this, Morty? It's going to make some of the folk mad."

"People are dying, like flies, Charles. We won't know for sure until we try it. I know it's going to be an expense but I don't believe we have a choice."

"Okay, bro. I'll call up the council in Rachel and see if they have enough water to go around. They have a water carrier. I'll also need to arrange with the store to bring in a lot more bottled water."

"Thanks, Charles. I'll make sure the supply from the reservoir is shut off."

Despite the results of the tests Mortimer felt a tinge of pride in his discovery of the correlation. It made him feel his contribution to the small community equaled that of his brother's. Since boys, the rivalry between them fostered an atmosphere of fierce competition, but Charles always came out on top. This time the sheriff of Hemlock might have hit the nail on the head and saved lives. He placed a call to the town's municipal handyman.

"Doug? I want you to shut off the town's water supply with immediate effect. I am drafting a quick bulletin to the Hemlock residents as to why we need to take this precaution."

"Sure thing, sheriff. I'll do it right away."

Mortimer started to type up a short notice.

\*

O'Malley waited for the two men to go their separate ways before he opened the vehicle's door and slipped out onto the concrete floor. He could see one of the men in the office, with his back to the window, a cup of coffee in hand. The other man continued to walk along the tunnel and could no longer be seen. O'Malley decided to follow the second man. He understood his time might be limited before they discovered his escape but an inquisitive nature drove him on to see what the military was up to. His gut told him Hangar-3 featured high on the list of clues which came to mind. He no longer had any doubt as to the involvement of General Watkins in what appeared to be a conspiracy, hidden in the confines of Hangar-3. The conversation between the two men alluded to "the old man", and that expression was exclusive to General Watkins.

A hundred yards down the tunnel he spotted the elevator station. He stopped to inspect the doors, with its security scanner access. A multitool would have made it an easy job to pry off the scanner's cover, for access to the electrics and gain use of the elevator. A slight cough from behind caused him to swivel around to face the danger. Adrenaline surged through his system as he prepared to lunge at the person, but instead, he froze.

"Maria? What in god's name are you doing here?"

"We need to find a safe place to talk before I explain," she said.

They walked together along the tunnel until a set of double doors appeared on the right. A sign read: "LAB". Each door possessed a small, high window and O'Malley took a quick glance.

"There is someone in there," he said.

Tam beckoned him to follow and they set off again. A few minutes later they came to a large single door with a sign: "Hardware Storage". She pushed the door open and peered into the room.

"Let's go in here, she said."

He followed her and a quick glance around the room revealed rows of wooden crates. They decided to move into an alcove which contained a desk, with two chairs. O'Malley couldn't contain himself.

"How did you get into this facility?"

Tam gave a brief explanation of what took place at the security. She heard an object being dragged past the cell and dumped into the four-by-four. At which point, Lieutenant Blake allowed her to leave.

"I knew you were in trouble, but you somehow seemed to have overcome that," she said.

He gave her a wan smile. "I need to make a confession—I'm not Mr. O'Malley, in charge of logistics and statistics; I'm a Special Agent with the FBI."

A glimmer of a smile appeared on Tam's face. "I know who you are, Dillon."

He looked at her aghast. "How in..."

She cut him off. "I have my own confession to make."

She stuck out her hand. "Tam Clyde-Walker, CIA. I received a call from my superior to inform me of your posting."

He grinned, grabbed her hand and shook it. "Well, it's sure good to make your acquaintance, Tam. Glad to have an ally in this godforsaken place."

"What do you know about the murder of Greenberg?" she asked

He told her about the adjutant's journal entries and what he saw in the level one office cabinet.

"It's possible Greenberg broke into level one and stumbled across the same documents in the office. I think they may have discovered him," said O'Malley.

She nodded. "There's something much bigger going on here than we can imagine. I was appointed to the case because the CIA received a tip about a secret operation, which might be against the national interests of the United States. We believe someone is developing a weapon which could be used to destroy millions of lives."

"For what reason?" O'Malley asked.

"We're not sure. It could be for control of the country, maybe the world, who knows?"

"The FBI was obviously not briefed on the matter but then that is typical posturing. I was sent in by our deputy director, whom I believe, was tipped off by someone here at Area 51."

"It doesn't matter," she said. "The problem currently belongs to us."

"I understand. You have my full cooperation, as I no doubt have yours."

"I know a way out," she said.

"Before we go I need to share something with you," said O'Malley. "I overheard two guys talking while I hid in the vehicle park. They intend to take me to Hemlock in the morning—to dispose of me. I have no doubt that the two missing scientists suffered a similar fate. Hemlock is tied up in this somehow."

Tam gave the news some consideration. "Hemlock, as you already know, is suffering some sort of virus outbreak. Medical scientists and forensic experts from Vegas can't find the cause. The story the town's folk are telling is that an alien presence is responsible."

"I'm not sure I really buy this alien crap," said O'Malley.

"Then let me tell you what I've just seen," said Tam.

She told him of the clinic on the bunker's second level and the strange creature called, Maguilor.

"If you remember, about twenty years ago an incident took place in the Arizona desert—when the citizens of Phoenix saw those lights above the city? The rumor is that the Air Force shot down an alien craft."

He nodded and smiled. "I saw a photo of it in a file in the level one office filing cabinet."

"Well it's one hundred percent true," said Tam. "The creature appears to be old and in failing health. It spoke a few words to me through some sort of translator strapped over its face."

"That's unbelievable—a real, live alien?"

"Saw it with my own eyes, and if we had the time I would take you down there and show you." she said.

"We don't have time, unfortunately. If anyone checks the storeroom they'll find out I've escaped. You said you knew of a way out?"

"It's the way I came in," she said. "But it will take some doing—climbing up a vent pipe to get out, I mean."

"Then, we had better be on the move," said O'-Malley.

Ж

# 11

## The Agents plan Ahead

Tam led O'Malley back to the level one ventilator. The military would soon find the compromised gauze of the outlet on level two. They would put two and two together and suspect an intruder.

"The first eight feet of the vent is horizontal and ends at a junction with the vertical, where the pipe leads down to the next level and also up to the surface," said Tam.

She pointed to the outlet. "Here it is. I had to cut this gauze and it totally blunted my multi-tool. I'll go first—it's a bit narrow on the horizontal but the vertical is wide enough and corrugated, to make climbing easy."

The two agents slithered along the horizontal to the junction, where they met with the vertical vent. Tam led the way and the ascent seemed easy for her. O'Malley on the other hand, a little bigger and heavier, struggled up the vertical section. The rubber soles of his shoes continued to slip on the sidewall corrugations and on several occasions, he lost his grip. After fifteen minutes they popped out the top of the pipe at ground level, both a little winded by the effort. O'Malley spotted the ventilator cap. He slid it back over the top of the pipe and began to insert the screws.

"Let's not make it easy for them to discover how I got out. They won't know about you at this stage," said O'Malley.

"I guess it won't take long for them to put two and two together. They're going to freak out when they realize someone has seen the alien."

"General Watkins is mixed up in this whole thing," said O'Malley. "Those two guys I told you about?—one of them mentioned the 'old man' would take care of you if you caused any trouble."

"My superior briefed me on the possibility and that's why Watkins knew nothing of my appointment," said Tam. "Lieutenant Blake also mentioned before he let me go, that I was welcome to go and see the general if I had any complaints about our arrest."

O'Malley glanced at the time. "It's 12:35 a.m. We have to either lie low somewhere, or get off the base—I would love to take a look at Hemlock, but it's at least twenty-five miles away."

Tam nodded. "One of our people is working in the Hemlock municipal office. I would love to follow up with her. I also have a colleague, here on the base who works in my department. He might help us—he's sent several signals he would love to get me into bed, but despite his overzealous sex drive, I think I can trust him."

"What does he do?" O'Malley asked.

"He's in charge of supplier's accounts and sometimes takes trips to Vegas to find better products—domestic supplies, not military."

"You mean food, cleaning materials and stuff like that?"

"Exactly. He's in a good position to take us through the gate without raising suspicion."

"What will you tell him?"

Tam gave the question some thought. "I'll tell him who I am but won't give away my real name, or why we're here—it's the only way I'll gain his cooperation and keep him quiet. I'll threaten him with legal action if he divulges what he knows."

O'Malley inserted the final screw in the ventilator cap. "I hope you're right. Let's go."

They jogged off toward the dormitories.

*

Captain Benson pulled out a file from a folder in the cabinet. The tag read, GROOM LAKE—AREA 51. He opened it, picked out a document and scanned to the footer, where he spotted the phone number of the desired contact. A "burner," or unregistered phone kept in the safe, would be used for the confidential conversation. Benson removed it and keyed in the number.

A gruff voice answered. "Why are you calling so late?"

"I'm sorry, sir, but I wanted to let you know it might be in our mutual interest if we stopped now —we have what we need. There has been a development, a new problem."

"What would that be?" asked the contact.

"I heard this evening that the town's water supply is going to be shut off and water will be trucked into Hemlock from outside." said Benson.

The contact responded. "Do you think they've cottoned on to what we're doing?"

"The sheriff discovered that people, who use bottled water for drinking purposes, were not affected by the Omega solution. Tobias has retested the water to allay any fears but the sheriff has decided to shut off the supply anyway until they can prove conclusively that the water is safe."

"So there's no point in making the last run. Is Clandecker happy with the latest test?"

"He feels we are a go, Sir. The product works, one hundred percent. "

"Okay, tell him to send me the final compound figures and I'll take it from there."

"Can I take it our business at this end is concluded?" asked Benson.

"You and Clandecker will receive payment as agreed when General Watkins gives the all clear, but you must make sure there is no further interference from the FBI agent."

"We have it in hand, Sir—don't worry about a thing. By midday tomorrow, O'Malley will no longer be a threat to Omega."

"I hope you're right, Captain."

Benson ended the call, leaned back in his chair and smiled.

\*

Tam knocked on the dorm door. She glanced appreciatively at O'Malley, cleaned up and with a change of clothing as they waited. The door opened and a surprised Henry stared out at them. He grinned and stepped aside.

"Maria, how nice of you to visit me." The smile disappeared, however, when he caught sight of O'Malley.

"Sorry to wake you up, Henry. I have an important matter to discuss with you. This is Special Agent O'Malley of the FBI." She stood aside and allowed O'Malley to enter the room. Henry looked taken aback.

"FBI? Oh, Christ—what have I done wrong?"

Tam placated him. "You've done nothing wrong, Henry. We need your help. I have a confession to make—I haven't been entirely honest with you. Although I work on the base, I'm not really employed by the military—I work for the CIA." She pulled her badge from the inside pocket of her windbreaker.

"Shit a brick," he said. "And I thought you were an innocent damsel needing male company."

Tam chuckled. "Not so innocent, I'm afraid, and I'm not adverse to male company. Special

Agent O'Malley and I are working on a case—it's classified so I can't tell you anything—but we need your help. The people we are investigating are after us and we need to get off the base. We want to follow up on some clues in Hemlock."

"Hemlock? Let me guess—you want me to drive you out there."

Tam buttered him up a little. "I knew you weren't just a pretty face, Henry."

"When do you want to go," he asked.

O'Malley glanced at his watch—1:30 am. "First light, so as not to raise any suspicions at the gate. Just tell them you're getting an early start on a drive to Vegas."

Henry gave the suggestion some thought. "I have a whole host of products, wrongly labeled by the supplier, which I said I would return next week. They're smaller boxes and include rubber mats for our gymnasiums—we can pack them in the back of my SUV, on top of the two of you. They never check through anything I take out, anymore."

"It's a deal then. We'll meet you at your vehicle at 6:00 am. You are not to tell anyone of this, understood?"

"I won't breathe a word on one condition." he gave her a crooked smile. "When this is all over you agree to a few drinks at Sam's Place."

"Agreed," she said. They shook hands and departed. The two agents took leave of each other and went back to their respective rooms.

*

At 6:00 am the next morning they met with Henry at the civilian parking lot, adjacent to the dorms and drove across to the Supply building. Henry unlocked the storeroom door and the three of them carried out a load of boxes on a four-wheeled dolly. They returned to the store for two medium sized gym mats and Henry checked his inventory sheet to confirm all the products marked for return. O'Malley and Tam crouched down in the wells of the backseat area and allowed Henry to place some mats over them, with smaller boxes, interspersed over the top. He placed two larger boxes in the trunk.

"Let's get going before we smother under all this crap," shouted Tam.

Henry drove to the gate and produced his credentials.

"Going back to Vegas, Henry?" said the guard, who recognized him from his previous excursions.

Henry sounded convincing. "Those idiots at Southport Supplies screwed up the order. All this stuff has to be returned—I don't mind spending the day in the big city, though."

"Get on your way then. Give my best to Vegas," said the guard.

Henry breathed a sigh of relief and drove through the gate. Ten miles further on, he pulled off the road and gave the two agents the opportunity to extricate themselves.

*

Captain Benson burst into level one's office, grabbed the phone and called Lieutenant Blake at Security. He glanced at his wristwatch—7:34 a.m.

"He's escaped. He's gone. We need to get onto this, now," shouted Benson. His voice contained a measure of panic.

"Who are you talking about, Sir?"

"O'Malley, you idiot. Get those goons of yours here pronto. He's loose in a highly classified area."

"Easy on, Sir," said Blake. "How did he manage that? He was shackled hand and foot."

"I don't know, Lieutenant. The cuffs are lying here, on the storeroom floor, unlocked. He must be some sort of Houdini."

"We'll be right down, Sir. Don't panic—we'll find him. It's a secure facility and there's no way out other than the main entrance."

"All I know is we must find him before he raises the alarm."

"We will find him, Sir. Hang tight—we'll be there in a few minutes."

Benson ended the call. He stepped outside the office and looked around frantically. No one could get out through the entrance gate without a security card and he assured himself that nobody could have slipped out when he and Clandecker drove into the bunker. A glance down past the recreation room, toward the laboratory, produced no sign of anyone, or a place to hide. The best-kept secrets in history lay on the levels below—accessible by a single elevator.

Benson mused within the turmoil of his mind and the churn of his gut. God forbid that O'Malley should stumble on the entrance to the floor below. He could not be allowed to escape the bunker at any cost.

A few minutes later the main entrance door opened and a four-by-four roared in to stop outside the storeroom. Lieutenant Blake and the two cammo-dudes jumped out, each with a weapon in hand. They joined Benson at the door of the storeroom and peered down at the cuffs, which lay on the floor.

"Blake looked at his watch. It's difficult to say when he escaped, but I put out an APB with the rest of base security and no one has seen him, so far."

"My concern, Lieutenant, is what he may see in the bunker if he by chance somehow bypasses the system."
"Of course, Sir. We'll conduct a search of this floor. We don't have clearance for the other floors.

"I'll search that area myself. You and your men take the entire top floor. Make sure you don't miss any possible hiding places."

Blake and the two dudes jogged off in the direction of the laboratory while Captain Benson followed. He stopped in front of the elevator station and pulled out a security card, which he slid through a scanner on the wall. The doors flew open and he descended to the second level. Once in the clinic, he did a quick check on Maguilor and noted that all appeared to be in order. The alien lay on his bed asleep, the cadence of his breathing slow, but consistent. Over several years the aliens managed to adjust to living conditions on Earth through a program of a gradual increase in the local breathable atmospheric content. Their planet of origin provided a much greater percentage of nitrogen in the mix and the program provided a gradual increase in oxygen. However, anatomically, they appeared to be very similar to human beings.

Benson looked around the room, conscious of the fact the clinic would not be accessible to anyone without a top secret clearance. His concerns, however, lay in O'Malley's abilities to overcome such obstacles. His eyes scanned the equipment and the room in general. A frown creased his brow when he saw the vent outlet.

# 12

## A Quick visit to Hemlock

Henry dropped Tam and O'Malley off at the largest hotel in Hemlock. But for the sparse, dry ground and its intermittent bushes, the town looked spectacular against the backdrop of the Groom Mountains. The clear sky promised another beautiful day, with temperatures warm enough for people to seek shade by 10:00 a.m.

O'Malley asked the hotel receptionist for two rooms.

"You'll have to speak to Sheriff Cranwell. All the hotels are closed at the moment," she advised. "The water has also been shut off and I believe they'll truck in a supply from outside. We appear to be under attack by aliens."

"Why do you think that," asked O'Malley.

The receptionist went off into a long explanation of the town's UFO history.

"It has to be a virus from outer space, or something similar," she concluded.

"Where do we find the sheriff?" asked Tam.

"You will find his office in Roswell Street. If you carry on down our road it's the main road through town, at the intersection." She pointed out the direction.

Tam and O'Malley set off on foot.

"She seemed quite spooked about the alien thing," he said.

"After what I saw last night I can believe her. What if the aliens have returned to take revenge?"

"By killing off a few of the town's people? I would think if they were serious about revenge it would be on a much grander scale. But I have to admit—the presence of the alien in the bunker and the photo of the crashed ship I saw in that file, sounds very convincing. I wonder if the military managed to repair the one they shot down in 1997."

O'Malley stared at her for a moment. "You may have a point. However, I saw the extent of the damage in the photo and I would have thought it to be beyond repair."

Fifteen minutes later they arrived at their destination and knocked on the door.

"There's always something cozy about these small villages," said O'Malley.

"Ghostly if you ask me," said Tam.

The door opened and a man in his mid-thirties stared out at them.
"Sheriff Cranwell?" asked O'Malley.

"Yes—I'm the sheriff. Please come in." He stepped aside and they entered. "Who are you folk and what brings you to Hemlock?"

Both Tam and O'Malley pulled out their respective badges. "Sheriff, we would like to ask a few questions, if we may."

"I wondered how long it would take the FBI to arrive on my doorstep but to have the CIA as well, is a bit overwhelming and intimidating," said the sheriff.

O'Malley asked if they could sit down and talk. Mortimer Cranwell relaxed a little and offered coffee. "I am using bottled water since we suspect our water supply may have been tampered with. I've always used bottled water, personally."

Cranwell gave them a brief rundown on his family's business, how it started and the history of the town. He told them how he awoke in the early hours one morning, to hear a vehicle travel through the town at high speed, and the terrible results which followed on the same day.

"Tell us about the water," asked Tam.

The sheriff told them about his questionnaire and discovery of the correlation between municipal and bottled water.

"Dr. Tobias, the head of medical forensics in Vegas, and chairperson of the Pathogenic and Dangerous Disease Action Group has had the water retested. The first and two consequent tests by the scientists proved the water to be safe to drink but when I came out with the correlation they decided to look at it again. They've discovered a residue which Tobias says could be the result of a dozen natural elements found in subterranean water. The tests appear inconclusive at the moment— so, we have decided to stop using the town's natural water supply until they prove conclusive. My brother, Charles has made arrangements for water to be brought in."

"I understand your brother is the town's mayor?" Tam asked.

"My brother is the smart one in the family. It's a job for which my father groomed him."

"How many people have died so far?" asked O'Malley.

"Thirty-eight and counting. A lot of the town's people wouldn't drink the water because it contains a lot of calcium and magnesium carbonates—very hard. If my theory proves to be correct the choice of bottled water has saved the lives of those who are still untouched by the disease."

"Sheriff—have you seen anything else which might be suspicious, or seen any people who might be deemed as such?"

"Other than the sound of that vehicle racing through town on each occasion, I can't say that I have."

"Do you think someone drove in during the night and deposited a foreign substance in the town's reservoir?" asked Tam.

"It's possible. The only problem is except for a strange residue, the water comes up clean when tested," answered the sheriff.

O'Malley dropped his chin. "We have it on good authority that those two scientists from the base were brought here to be disposed of."

Cranwell looked shocked and became defensive. "I don't know anything about that. Hemlock's a sleepy little place that promotes the UFO business. We don't advocate disposing of people."

"Relax, sheriff. We're not accusing you, or the town's people, of anything," said Tam. "CIA intelligence has also confirmed that two men from the base come here quite often to have a drink at the pub. They disappear for a while into a back room to meet with someone and we were wondering who that person may be?"

Sheriff Cranwell gave the question some thought. "I know some of the folk from the base come here on the odd occasion. I don't drink much, personally—however, I have been called in a few times when arguments break out between patrons. I can't say I've noticed any unfamiliar persons."

The door opened and a man walked in. He saw O'Malley and Tam. "I'll come back when you're not busy, bro."

Mortimer beckoned to the man. "Come in, Charles. Meet our visitors."

The sheriff introduced the two agents to his brother. Charles smiled and stuck out his hand.

O'Malley offered his chair but Charles Cranwell declined it.

"What brings the FBI and CIA to our doorstep?" Charles asked.

O'Malley elaborated on their conversation with the sheriff. "We're just saying that two people from the base often come to Hemlock for drinks at the pub. We would have thought that with the military's aversion to the proximity of the town, and the town's promotion of the UFO business, the base people would not be welcome."

The mayor's eyes narrowed. "We don't turn anyone away unless they have bad intentions. Despite Hemlock's controversial presence, we've never experienced a problem with any of the military personnel—not that I know of."

O'Malley's gut suggested that Charles appeared uncomfortable with their presence. He decided not to push the envelope. He looked over at Tam, then at the sheriff.

"I understand you have a state of emergency on at the moment. We haven't concluded our business in the area yet, so we're asking your permission to stay in one of the hotels until we have questioned some of the residents."

Mortimer nodded. "I appreciate your attitude. I realize you could pull rank and demand to stay, and there would be nothing we could do about it. Of course, you can stay. I will call the receptionist at the Sunset Rest."

"Thanks, Sheriff. We won't need to stay too long—is your supermarket open?"

Charles chipped in. "If you're interested in the forensic matters of the case I can arrange for a meeting with Dr. Tobias, or you can go down to our sports field where the field hospital has been set up."

Tam stood and reached over to shake the sheriff's hand. "Thanks for the cooperation, sheriff." She turned to Charles. "Don't worry about setting up a meeting. We'll get down to the sports field as soon as we've booked into the hotel."

"I have arranged for water to be trucked in from Rachel. We'll have the reserve tanks at each hotel filled by this evening. Since I didn't see an official vehicle outside, how did you guys get here?" Charles asked.

O'Malley gave a quick answer. "Our vehicle gave trouble this morning so we came over with someone from the base. He'll pick us up again, to-morrow."

The mayor looked at them with a measure of suspicion but said nothing further and they left.

As they walked in the direction of the hotel O'-Malley shared his thoughts.

"What did you think?"

"I think the sheriff seemed genuinely surprised when we shared our intelligence report. The may-or, however, appeared a little cagey."

"I agree. I think he's trying to cover something up," said O'Malley.

"Or, he's just scared."

Five minutes later the sheriff pulled up in his truck. "Hop in—I'll give you a ride to the hotel."

Ж

# 13

## A Visit to the Field Hospital

The Sunset Rest Hotel provided a good view of the mountains and accommodated one hundred people. O'Malley and Tam each booked a separate room and were told about the water situation. They would not be able to take a shower until the first truckload of water arrived to fill the auxiliary tank.

A quick walk to the supermarket took a few minutes and when they arrived a "closed" sign hung on the door. O'Malley banged on the glass window and seconds later a man appeared.

"We're closed until the sheriff says we can re-open," said the man.

O'Malley pulled out his badge. "We need some supplies. We've just spoken to the sheriff. Are you the owner?"

The man's eye's bulged when he saw the credentials and he nodded. "Sure thing. Help yourself to what you need and I'll open up the cash register."

They each bought some toiletry items and O'-Malley asked the owner for a case of bottled water. "We're almost completely sold out. The mayor said he has arranged for a truckload to be here tomorrow."

"The mayor has arranged it—not you, yourself?"

The owner grinned. "Charles is a useful guy. He virtually owns the town. He has shares in the bottled water company, so he can pull strings for me."

O'Malley glanced at Tam. "He has shares in the company?"

The owner tried to make it sound more positive. "The Cranwell's, like my own family, are health nuts—plus he's an exceptional businessman."

"I hear there might be something wrong with the main water supply?"

"It's not confirmed yet but we aren't taking any chances," said the owner.
O'Malley rubbed his chin. "I see. Well, thank you for your time, Sir."

They paid for the purchases and walked back to the hotel.

"Charles Cranwell has shares in the bottling company," echoed Tam.

"Seems a bit convenient but I doubt if that would be enough reason to poison the water supply."

"Maybe not, but it may be a convenient supplement to the real crime," she said.

O'Malley grinned. "My, but you are the suspicious one."

Tam laughed and gave him a playful punch on the shoulder. He gave her a slight shove from behind and they both giggled like two children on the school playground.

Later in the morning, they made their way down to the sports field. The majority of beds in the main marquee were empty. A woman with a stethoscope around her neck approached them as they entered the tent.

"Can I help you?" she asked.

O'Malley made the introductions and produced his badge. The doctor introduced herself as Doctor Meyer.

"We were wondering if Dr. Tobias is on the site?" asked O'Malley.

She pointed to the other end of the marquee. "If you go out that entrance you'll see a tent on the left."

They thanked her and walked toward the back entrance. Four beds were occupied with people on life-support. Tam stopped to check one of them, a woman in her late forties. She whispered to O'Malley. "This woman is Sheila Graves. She is one of our contacts—the one who has been acquiring information here at Hemlock, for us."

"Is she CIA?" asked O'Malley.

"No. She's a contractor. We make extensive use of them."

O'Malley shook his head, "So sad."

Tam called Dr. Meyer over. "What is the status of this person's condition?"

Dr. Mayer looked at a screen and then at the chart. "She's in the final stages. No one affected has so far survived this epidemic"

Tam thanked her and they moved on out of the marquee. A smaller tent on the left with a sign, "Admin", caught their attention and O'Malley placed his hand on Tam's forearm. "This is it."

He opened the flap and peered inside. An older man in a white coat looked up and removed his glasses. "Do you need help?"

"Dr. Tobias?"

The man nodded and O'Malley, once again, flashed his badge and made the introductions.

"We have been speaking to the sheriff and he tells me there is a possible connection between all these deaths and the water supply.

Dr. Tobias scratched his bald head. "There may be, but it's not conclusive."

The doctor went on to share his opinion.

"There is a residue which could be the result of a combination of things found in all subterranean water supplies."

"Do you believe that the origin of that element might be from an alien source?" Tam asked.

Tobias chuckled. "I doubt it, Miss Clyde-Walker. I know there are rumors of an alien presence in the area but that's all they are—unsubstantiated rumors."

O'Malley inclined his head. "If the cause did lie with the water supply where do you think such an element might have been introduced?"

Tobias considered the notion. "It would have to be directly into the reservoir, I would think, however, that's not my area of expertise."

O'Malley posed one final question. "What are the symptoms?"

"Catastrophic failure of major organs, followed by death."

"Thank you, Dr. Tobias. If we have any further questions we'll be in touch. How long do you intend to stay here?" O'Malley asked.

"Until the epidemic comes to an end, or we find the source."

O'Malley and Tam left the tent and walked back through the marquee. They said goodbye to Dr. Meyer and left for the hotel.

As they walked O'Malley became conscious of Tam's closeness. Every now and then their arms would touch and he could see her out of the corner of his eye. She would cast an occasional glance in his direction. An attraction between them could become a complication. The need, however, for love and affirmation within him overcame the conflict. Tam's beautiful, trim body heightened his sexual desire and she appeared to be available. His marriage to Janet teetered on the brink. After years of psychological conflict and the recent affair with a colleague in his previous assignment, the relationship had sustained extensive damage. O'Malley wondered if he might face a similar challenge with Tam's presence.

"Penny for your thoughts?" she asked.

'That proverbial penny has become very inflated," he answered.

Tam smiled and gripped his upper arm. He could feel the touch of her skin against his own and it felt good. A sudden sensation of self-consciousness overtook him. "I think I might need a shower—this heat brings out the worst in me."

She laughed and placed her head on his shoulder. "We're both in the same boat, Dillon. Maybe we can overcome that problem together?"

He grinned and the self-consciousness disappeared. "Maybe we can," he said.

They heard the sound of a truck approaching from behind and O'Malley turned to look over his shoulder. His gut sensed something out of the ordinary. The black color of the vehicle made it look like a hearse, and for a moment he chided himself on his sense of paranoia. Tam also heard the vehicle and he felt her body stiffen. She too turned her head to look, as it roared toward them at speed.

At twenty yards a shadowy figure opened the rear cab window and to their horror, the barrel of a gun appeared. A flame of fire spat from the muzzle. O'Malley's reaction came the moment he saw the window slide down. In a flash, the glock revolver appeared in his hand and he shoved Tam away from him as he swiveled, knelt down and took aim, all at the same time.

"Get down," he shouted.

Bullets sprayed around them as they both hit the deck. The Glock's muzzle flamed and the 9 mm projectiles smashed into the side of the truck's door and broke the rear cab window as the vehicle passed by. He became conscious of additional fire and turned to see Tam on her stomach, down on the ground, firing away with her own pistol. The truck did not stop but raced off at high speed. O'-Malley turned to look behind him. Tam lay on the ground with a pained expression on her face. She clutched at one of her legs and rolled over in an attempt to stand.

He jumped up and ran to her.

"Are you okay? Were you hit?" His voice sounded hoarse.

She nodded. "My leg—upper right thigh. I think it's only a flesh wound, though."

O'Malley checked her leg. He tore the pants material in order to get a better view of the damage.

"Careful—I'll sue you for a new pair," she joked.

"How does it feel?"

"Like hell—burning a bit, but I'll be okay."

He helped her stand. "Can you place any weight on it?"

She tried to lean on the leg and almost fainted. O'Malley grabbed her, placed her arm around his neck and shoulder for support and moved off in the direction of the hotel.

He vented his anger at the people in the truck. "Bastards."

It took a while for them to get back to the hotel, where a horrified receptionist helped O'Malley get Tam up to her room.

"Do you need a doctor?" she asked.

"Just bring me your first-aid kit," he demanded. She nodded and disappeared.

He lay Tam down on the bed and pulled her jeans off. He grabbed a wad of toilet paper and applied it to the wound, which looked grisly, but as he cleared away the blood did not appear to be that bad. The receptionist returned with the kit.

"This is all we have," she said. "Should I call the sheriff?"

"Yes. I think that might be a good idea, thanks."

After the receptionist left the room O'Malley cleaned Tam's wound and dressed it as best he could. It looked okay, but he discerned she might need painkillers from the pharmaceutical section in the supermarket.

He called the receptionist. "Ask the sheriff to bring some painkillers from the Pharmacy. Tell him I'll pay for them."

He pulled a blanket over Tam and made her comfortable. She ogled him through half-opened eyes and he could see the effects of shock as she focused on his face.

"Thanks, Dillon. I presume you didn't have your way with me while I was in Lalaland?"

He grinned. "I felt tempted but all the blood put me off."

"How does it look?" she asked.

"You're going to be fine. It looks okay. The receptionist is calling the sheriff and he'll bring some pain-killers."

She grabbed his hand and he leaned down to kiss her forehead.

She closed her eyes. "I've wanted you to do that for a while now," she said.

Ж

# 14

## Spilled Milk

Robin Clandecker and Captain Benson discussed the morning's discovery. The escalation of tension between them became palpable. After a time of cussing each other out with accusations and exaggerated threats, a sudden calm intervened as both realized the implications of O'Malley's escape.

"So, what are we going to do?" asked Benson.

"We have to let the old man know—he'll take care of it, somehow."

"He's going to blow several gaskets when he hears Maguilor has been compromised," answered Benson.

Clandecker wiped the perspiration off his brow with the back of his hand. "This could have serious consequences."

"Too bad. It's spilled milk and it needs to be cleaned up. At least we know how he got out and we also know he is somewhere on this base, in hiding. Blake is conducting a full search as we speak," said Benson.

"When will you let the old man know what's happened?"

"I'll wait to see if Blake can find him first. No reason to rattle the old man's cage unless it's necessary." The captain fiddled with an epaulet button. "We know all the possible hiding places on the base."

'What about the MacDonald woman? Do you think she might be mixed up in this?"

"Blake will check out where she is and what she's doing. The old man will take care of her if she becomes a problem."

"I hope you're right, Ian. I'm going back downstairs—keep me informed."

*

O'Malley, revolver in hand, placed his eye against the peephole in response to the short rap on the door. He let the sheriff in and set his glock down on the dresser. The sheriff appeared rattled by the escalating circumstances.

"Is your colleague alright?" He looked down at Tam with concern.

"I'm going to be fine, thank you, Sheriff," said Tam. She pulled herself up into a sitting position. "It's just a flesh wound."

"Did you manage to get a look at the person who shot at you?"

"No—everything happened so quickly. Our prime response was to find cover and return the fire."

"Here are your pain-killers. Don't worry about the money."

"Thanks," said O'Malley. He grabbed the packet, opened it and pulled out a container with tablets. "I'll get some water."

The sheriff stood and donned his hat. "I must get back to the station. I'll let you know if I find anything conclusive about the black truck. In the meantime, stay off that leg."

"Thanks, Sheriff," said Tam.

O'Malley moved to the door and opened it. "We'll also be in touch if we find out what's going on. We always like to have the cooperation of local law enforcement."

The sheriff nodded and left.

"What do you think?" asked O'Malley.

"It seems as though he wants to help. I'm not sure if he's hiding anything."

He opened the door again. "It's lunchtime—I'm hungry. Can I get you anything?"

"No, I'm good—just feeling a bit tired; those pills are beginning to take effect."

"I'll go down to the pub and see what they have to eat. Keep your firearm handy and don't open the door for anyone," he said.

O'Malley made his way down to the pub. With no tourists left in town the place appeared to be empty, so he rang the bell on the bar counter. A moment later a younger man stuck his head through an inter-leading doorway.

"Be with you in a second." The face disappeared and he heard a short conversation take place in a back room. The young man re-appeared.

"Sorry about that. The town's almost empty and I wasn't expecting any visitors—what can I get you?"

"Do you have any pub lunches?"

"Kitchen's closed but I'll ask my wife to rustle up something for you—she's the receptionist."

O'Malley thanked the man and asked for a beer to drink while he waited. The receptionist appeared after a few minutes. "Oh, it's you, Special Agent—will a ham and cheese sandwich do?" she asked.

"Anything will hit the spot at the moment."

"How's your friend doing?"

"She's okay. Just needs some rest," said O'Malley.

The receptionist scurried off to make him a sandwich while her husband brought the beer.

"You live here in Hemlock?" asked O'Malley.

"Yes—Tess and I have been here for about six years now. We love the place. My name's John, by the way, and I believe you work for the FBI?" he stuck out his hand.

"Dillon O'Malley, Special Agent." he shook John's hand. "You tend the bar here by yourself?"

"I have a relief who comes in on weekends to give me a break, but I'm pretty much here most of the time."

"My colleague says she heard that two guys come here quite regularly from the base and they sometimes meet with someone in an inter-leading room."

John pointed to a door in the adjacent wall. "We have a legal gambling room where patrons can play a few slot machines and have a game of poker."

"Do you know who these men might be?"

"That would be Mr. Clandecker and Captain Benson. They come once or twice a month, have a few beers and enjoy a game of cards."

"Do you know if they meet with anyone specifically?"

"I go in only when they call for drinks. I've seen them with different people."

"Would any of those people be the sheriff or the mayor?" asked O'Malley.

"The sheriff doesn't drink and the only time he comes here is if there's an altercation or problems with one of the tourists. The Mayor, Charles Cranwell, however, does come on the odd occasion."

O'Malley sipped on his beer. "Did you ever see Cranwell talking to Clandecker or Benson?"

"Yes—they seem to have arranged a regular game of poker for each month-end."

The secretary brought the sandwich. "Sorry, Special Agent. I sent the cook home to Vegas until things get back to normal, so there are no pub meals until further notice. I usually cook dinner for my hubby and I'd be happy to make extra for you and Miss Clyde-Walker."

That's very kind of you," answered O'Malley. "We'll take you up on that—I'm just not sure how long we'll be here."

"Let me know by 5:30 each evening and I'll make extra portions. Sorry, have to get back to the desk—the phone's ringing off the hook. People are wanting to know when they can return."
O'Malley thanked her and tucked into the sandwich. John hovered around not sure if there would be any more questions. O'Malley did have one more thing to ask.

"Do you know anyone in Hemlock who owns a modern, black pickup truck?"

John gave the question some consideration. "I don't think anyone in the village owns such a vehicle. They're mostly old, beat up jobs used for off-road riding. However, I believe Mr. Clandecker at the military base, has such a vehicle."

O'Malley's raised his eyebrows. "Clandecker—the civilian scientist who works at the base?"

"Yeah. He came to show it off about two weeks ago."

O'Malley finished his sandwich and drained the last of his beer. "Thanks, John. You've been most helpful. I need to check on my colleague but I'm sure she'll be famished by dinner time, so please tell your wife we'll pop down for a bite. What would be a good time?"

"7:00 p.m. would be fine. I'll tell Tess."

O'Malley left the bar and walked back up the stairs, to the top floor. At the top of the steps, he looked out of an adjacent window, which looked down on the carpark. A vehicle pulled in and two people got out. O'Malley's blood ran cold—the tall cammo-dude and his sidekick, the same men who apprehended him and Tam on the service road the night before.

He ran to Tam's room, inserted the keycard to open the door and peered into the room—she lay on her back, asleep, with her head tilted to one side. He decided to leave her, go back to the reception and if the dudes came in to ask the receptionist about them, he would be able to decide on a course of action. The dudes would have known about the town's state of emergency and the shutdown of facilities. It meant their purpose for a visit to Hemlock would not be a recreational one.

O'Malley reached the ground floor before the two men walked into the reception. A vending machine stood at the bottom of the stairwell and afforded him a place to hide for a good view of the reception. The receptionist sat at her desk, busy with a phone call and did not see the two men until they stopped at the service counter. She glanced up and motioned for them to wait while she completed her conversation. O'Malley noticed the dudes both carried firearms in holsters, attached to their belts. With her call completed, she turned to the dudes. "Can I help you, gentlemen?"

"We want to know if two people booked in here this morning—a man and a woman."

"Why do you ask?" She looked at them with suspicion.

"We're on military business and need to talk to them," said the tall dude.

"They're in rooms 204 and 206, up the stairs and on the second floor."

The dude thanked her and the two men moved toward the stairwell, where O'Malley hid behind the vending machine. He pulled out the glock, slipped into the stairwell and took the stairs to the top floor. The element of surprise remained a factor as he raced down the hallway to Tam's room, inserted the keycard and slipped inside. Tam still slept, unaware of the unfolding drama.

# 15

## The Cranwell Brothers

Charles and Mortimer Cranwell, engaged in a heated conversation, eyed each other over the desk. The two brothers seldom argued.

"Dammit, Charles. I can't order them about—they're law enforcement officers who carry far greater authority than I do."

"Bullshit, Morty. You're the sheriff of Hemlock and no one has more right to intervene in the town's affairs than you do."

"But, we don't have anything to hide and I can't stop them asking questions."

Charles jutted out his chin. "Think about it, bro. They work for the government. I tell you they are here to put blame on Hemlock's municipal management for the deaths of all these people."

Mortimer looked down at his hands. "We haven't done anything wrong, Charles. We look after the town's interests. We promote business for the local community and I look after the law side of things as best as I can. The agents have actually been very friendly and supportive."

"Don't be taken in, bro. They have a hidden agenda. I have it on good authority they plan to exploit the situation. They intend to make a case so that Hemlock will have to close down—where do you think that leaves us? We've borrowed heavily from the bank over the last few years, in order to keep things going."

Mortimer's exasperation spilled over. "What do you expect me to do?"

"I want you to start acting like you're the sheriff of this place. Don't give those two glorified police officers a thing, and cooperate only to a point. We must protect our investment. The military would also love to see us go—we've been a thorn in their side for years."

"Okay, Charles. I see your point but I don't necessarily agree that the government is out to screw us over."

"We mustn't give the government anything which can be misconstrued. I would imagine the FBI and the CIA are looking for a reason to solve this mystery quickly and they don't particularly care who takes the blame."

Mortimer sighed. "I'll do what I can. By the way, did you know someone shot at the agents from a pickup today?"

Charles looked surprised. "No, I didn't. Who would do such a thing?"

"I haven't a clue. Someone in a modern, black pickup drove by them as they were walking from the sports field to the hotel. The woman was hit in the leg."

Charles gave the matter some thought and chuckled. "Maybe it's a good thing. Perhaps they'll pack up and get out of our town."

Mortimer did not find his answer amusing. "Shit, Charles—how can you say such a thing? She might have been killed."

"Not our problem, Morty. They shouldn't be here, however, I wonder who else has taken umbrage at their presence."

"Charles? You didn't..."

"Cancel that thought bro. You know that's not my style," said Charles.

Mortimer relaxed. "No, you're right. Guess I'm getting a bit jumpy."

Charles stood to go. "I must get back to my office. Remember, bro. Do not give them anything that could jeopardize our position."

Mortimer stared at his brother but held his tongue.

*

O'Malley stood at the door and waited for the dudes to make their appearance at the top of the stairwell. He peeked around the doorjamb, the glock held in both hands in typical military stance. The tall dude stepped from the top stair onto the second-floor landing, into the corridor, with his service revolver drawn. The sidekick followed on behind him, also with a gun in hand.

"Stop right there," shouted O'Malley.

The two men stopped in their tracks and froze.

"What do you guys want? What're you doing here?" asked O'Malley.

The tall dude lowered his gun. "We've come to discuss something with you, O'Malley."

"After your actions last night I didn't think we would have anything to discuss."

O'Malley saw the other dude step backward toward the stairwell. He knew the man would try to climb up the outside onto the balcony and glanced over his shoulder at the sliding door. Tam stirred in her sleep but did not wake up as the painkillers took their toll.

"Don't try anything," shouted O'Malley. "I'll cut you down."

"Relax, O'Malley. We just want to talk. There's no reason for anyone to start shooting."

"Talk, I'm listening," said O'Malley. He tried to keep his attention in two places at once. He expected the other dude to appear on the balcony, outside the room and try to take him by surprise, while the tall dude kept him occupied.

"We seem to have had a misunderstanding yesterday," said the man.

"A misunderstanding?" said O'Malley. "You call locking us in a cell, smashing in the back of my head and throwing me into the storeroom, a misunderstanding?"

"Yeah, the boss made a mistake. We were supposed to pick up someone else and you just got in the way."

A sudden crash of glass came from the sliding door and a projectile thudded against the opposite wall of the room. At the same time, the tall dude dropped to his knee and began firing at O'Malley. The bullets thunked into the top of the doorway, close to his head. He ducked back into the room and closed the door, but discovered a new threat. The projectile lay on the floor and smoke started to billow out of it at a rate which filled the room within seconds. He heard Tam scream, her mind confused by all the sudden noise. O'Malley rushed over to the bed to protect her but never made it. A toxic agent, mixed into the smoke, caused him to lose consciousness and his last thought focused on his stupidity. He fell over Tam's legs and lay still. She too succumbed to the gas and fell backward, onto the pillow.

The tall cammo-dude entered the room, a gas mask strapped onto the lower half of his face. After opening the windows he surveyed the scene. The other dude joined him and together they dragged the inert bodies down the stairs, past the horrified receptionist and her bartender husband, out to the four-by-four. After a minute the receptionist regained her composure, shot behind her desk and picked up the phone.

"Sheriff? You had better come quickly. Some men have just taken the two agents away by force."

*

O'Malley awoke with a sudden jerk. His head felt as though it might split apart. In an instant, he knew the extent of their trouble. These were tough, hard men with possible service in Iraq, or Afghanistan, and they were used to killing people. There would be no mercy, a thought which spawned a sudden fear in him—they may have been the ones who disposed of Greenberg and the two scientists. O'Malley overheard a conversation which alluded to his removal to Hemlock, but as he thought about it, a place near the town might have been implied.

With a return to consciousness, feeling coursed back into stiff limbs and he became aware of another person—Tam. He tried to move his hands and feet, but as before, cuffs prevented it. She lay with her back to him and as if by appointment, she moved and tried to roll over to face him. Tam grunted as pain flooded her body but with an effort, she managed to face him.

For a brief moment, they looked into each other's eyes and O'Malley tried to convey an apology for their predicament. The gags stuffed into their mouths prevented any verbal conversation.

The road became bumpy and the driver changed down into four-wheel drive. By the incline and roughness of the track, O'Malley gathered they were up in the mountains. The vehicle bumped and jarred their bodies until it leveled out and came to a stop. The dudes jumped out and moved to the back of the vehicle. Their boots crunched on the rough gravel as they walked on rough gravel and when one of them opened the hatch-door, O'-Malley could feel a coolness in the air. The Cammo-dude pulled at O'Malley's feet, slid him out of the vehicle and allowed his body to fall onto the ground. Tam, also extricated in a rough manner, cried out in pain as her wounded leg scraped along the floor.

The taller of the dudes pulled out his cellphone and made a call. After a brief conversation, he turned to his buddy. "Let's get on with it."

"Can't we have some fun with her, first?" asked the smaller dude.

"We don't have time. The captain is waiting for us—move your ass."

The two men lifted their victims and each took their burden with a grunt.

Colin Setterfield

"Couldn't you have got closer?" complained the smaller dude. Tam tried to squirm loose, but he held her with a firm grip.

"Shut your trap. It's only another hundred yards to the top."

Both the men were young and strong. They bore their respective loads with relative ease.

*

Mortimer Cranwell muttered to himself as he pulled into the hotel parking. The situation with regards to the two agents and the military did not seem right. His brother, Charles, thought the two agents worked on the side of the military but the hotel receptionist indicated that two cammo-dudes took them away by force. Why would the military treat O'Malley and Clyde-Walker in such a way if they were on the same side?

He parked his pickup and ran into the reception where he found the distraught receptionist, with her husband, John.
"Thank God, you're here, Sheriff. You must do something for that poor couple."

"What exactly happened," the sheriff asked.

168

John and Tess told him about the battle between O'Malley and the dudes. They also showed him the damage done to Tam's room and how the two agents were carried out, unconscious, cuffed hand and foot.

"Did you see which way they went?"

John handed his wife another tissue from behind the counter. "They didn't go back to the base. You can still see the dust from their vehicle hanging in the air, over there."

He pointed toward a road which led up into the mountains.

Sheriff Cranwell frowned. "That road becomes a track and really doesn't lead anywhere."

Tess interjected. "It eventually ends at that deep gorge. I think it's called George's Pit."

"That's right. Charles and I were forbidden to play there when we were kids. I think it was first discovered by my grandfather, George Cranwell."

"Why would those men take the agent's there?" asked John.

The truth staggered Mortimer. "The hole is a narrow chasm which drops deep into the mountain side. No one knows how deep it is. I had better get going—there's no time to waste."

He shot out of the reception and jumped into his truck. John and Tess stared at the pickup as it roared out of the lot, into the road and raced off in the direction of the mountains.

# 16

## O'Malley and Tam

General Watkins scowled at the men who sat opposite him. Both averted their gaze. The general's face became flushed with anger as he pulled a handkerchief from his pocket and wiped the perspiration from his brow.

"How did he get away? How is it that I can't trust any of you with the simple task of containing one FBI agent? You took him to the one place he should never have been allowed to see, and he escapes while in your custody."

"We still don't know how he got out of the cuffs, Sir. I've had word that Miss MacDonald joined him and they're both in Hemlock this morning. We're still trying to work out how they got through the gate—someone helped them and we have our suspicions who it might be."

"All it means is there are more people who need to be dealt with. This is fast becoming a fiasco. It must be contained," shouted the general.

Lieutenant Blake spoke up. "I have two of my contractors, as we speak, following up in Hemlock, Sir. They're confident the problem will be dealt with."

General Watkins glared at him. "I hope you can trust those cammo-dudes, Lieutenant. If they bungle it this time I'll have your hide."

"We'll have it all sewn up by the end of the day, Sir," said Blake.

"What about the MacDonald woman?"

Captain Benson shifted in his seat. "We believe she might have met O'Malley on the plane from Vegas, General. Clandecker and I saw them having dinner together, yesterday evening before the two dudes arrested them. I've checked into her hire and there doesn't appear to be anything suspicious about it. I thought there was just a mutual attraction."

"—but she joins him after he escapes from Hangar-3," shouted the general. "She has to be more than just romantically involved."

Blake's phone rang. "Permission to take this, General. It's one of the dudes."

The general nodded and Blake walked to the back end of the office to take the call. He returned with a satisfied smile.

"They have O'Malley and Miss MacDonald in custody, Sir. It turns out Miss MacDonald isn't who she said she was. Her name is Tammy Clyde-Walker and she works for the CIA. They found her badge next to the bed. I've told the dudes to make sure there'll be no trace found of either of them."

"For Christ's sake. Is this never going to end? I purposely agreed to the placing of an agent here after Greenberg raised his concerns with the FBI's deputy director. Now the CIA is in on it, too?"

"We can testify to their leaving the base together, Sir. You were going to arrange for someone to stand in as O'Malley—let's do the same for Clyde-Walker."

The general relaxed. "Yeah, it should work, I guess. When the FBI and the CIA come looking for their personnel we just stick to our story. They left together and returned to Vegas."

*

O'Malley's body felt sluggish and cold in the cool, mountain air. He could feel the wind against his face as he lay on his back and looked up at the cloudless sky. The tall cammo-dude lifted the 200-pound dead-weight of the agent's body with little difficulty. In his mid-thirties and physical prime of life, the dude enjoyed the physicality of the exercise. It topped off what would be a day of excitement for him and his colleague. He taunted his friend and made a joke about unfit cammo-dudes who wallowed in the shadows of mediocrity and who needed a lot more training, to accomplish the peak fitness of the typical prime, male specimen.

"You're lagging behind—move your ass. She's only a light-weight."

His colleague shouted an obscenity and shared his own opinion. "Well said, by a gorilla who drinks gasoline and eats bricks for breakfast."

The men toiled up the incline until it leveled out, at which point they stopped for a short rest. The smaller dude dropped Tam onto the hard ground and she grunted in pain and indignation.

"Did you hear that?" asked the tall dude.

"What?"

"I thought I heard a vehicle."

"The wind's blowing a gale. You may have heard something that's far off—on the main drag."

"You're probably right. This area is pretty desolate," said the tall dude.

He pointed to Tam. "You might as well remove her gag—there's no one out here to hear anything."

He allowed O'Malley to fall off his shoulders as the smaller man pulled the gag out of Tam's mouth. He gave her a crooked smile. "Wake up, darling. The time has come for you to meet your maker."

Tam lay on her back and stared up at him in silence. A look of pain and disappointment registered in O'Malley's eyes. She nodded her head in an effort to convey that she understood. All law enforcement agents knew such a time might come. Their jobs placed them in constant danger and they all made a conscious choice to be involved, despite the possibility of death as an end result. Everyone faced death at the end of their lifetime and she entertained no regrets. Her captor attempted to taunt her and she determined to not give in to fear.

"So, you work for the CIA. I would never have thought you were the type." The smaller dude continued to test her. "Why don't we have a little fun?" He reached down between her legs.

Tam felt mortified but knew she could not prevent the assault. "You'll die in hell, you bastard," she screamed.

She tried to kick with her legs and roll away as he tried to grope her.

The tall dude did not remove O'Malley's gag. He watched his colleague with amusement and after a few more moments, commented. "Come on, fun's over—we must get on with it."

The smaller dude looked disappointed. "I was just beginning to have fun," he said.

They shouldered the bodies again and moved off toward the ledge, which overlooked George's Pit. It took another five minutes to reach the end of the track. The men dropped their loads and gazed out across the chasm before them. George's Pit, below, appeared deep and dark, a legacy of the Earth's violent past.

"Perfect place, isn't it?" said the tall dude.

The smaller man turned to Tam, who lay on her side. "You're going to join those two scientists down there."

"So you did kill those men," she shouted.

He pointed at the pit. "Don't worry, darling. It'll be quick."

Fear coursed through her body and any restraint, managed prior to their arrival at the gorge, disappeared. Tears began to roll down her cheeks, but she refused to give the dudes the satisfaction of knowing her fear. The dude leaned down and grabbed her shoulders. She tried to squirm away but the cuffs hindered her movements. O'Malley started to grunt and shake his head as the cammo-dude dragged Tam toward the ledge.

*

Sheriff Cranwell drove hard on the gravel road until it ran out and morphed into a track. He engaged the pickup's four-wheel drive, dropped to a snail's pace and proceeded up the bumpy incline. At the top of the hill, about a mile ahead, he saw the four-by-four parked and brought his truck to a stop. With the side window down and a pair of binoculars from the glove compartment in hand, he scanned the area but saw no one. The track further on crested a hill and disappeared from view.

Mortimer recognized the spot as he knew it well from his youth. George's Pit would be another one hundred yards beyond the hill's crest. A chill went down his spine as he thought of the cammo-dude's intentions. They would not take to his presence with any kindness, but he couldn't allow any murders on his watch. He drove until he felt the noise from the truck might carry to the men's ears, and then stopped. The sheriff took a rifle off the rack in the back window, left the truck and jogged up the path toward the four-by-four. After a quick investigation of the empty vehicle, he moved on.

A few minutes later the sheriff crested the hill and looked down the slight decline to the end of the track. The ledge at the footpath's end provided a platform for a panoramic view of a narrow gorge and provided a magnificent view of the adjacent mountain. He and Charles would lie on their stomachs and look over that ledge into George's Pit and experience the strong sense of vertigo it brought. He would often lie awake at night and think about how reckless they were as children, with Charles always the fearless one.

In the distance, he saw two men at the ledge. Both stood with hands on hips and looked out across the Pit. Mortimer trained the binoculars on the scene and saw the two agents on the ground, side by side, at the men's feet. The men were at least a hundred and fifty yards distant from his position on the crest of the hill. He hesitated and thought of a course of action. If he shouted at them it would give his presence away and remove the element of surprise.

They might, in haste do the evil deed before he could stop it, or they might also open fire on him. The moments passed interminably, but the situation took a quick change when one of the dudes grabbed an agent by the shoulders and started to drag the body toward the edge. He realized he could not wait for a second longer and lifted the rifle to take aim at the man's upper torso.

Sheriff Cranwell never thought he might have to kill another human being. He did not even consider himself to be a good shot.

# 17

## Sheriff Cranwell

The dude dragged Tam's body to within three feet of the ledge. She squirmed and fought, but the cuffs prevented any attempts at escape. O'Malley's eyes bulged as he tried to worm his body toward Tam's, his mind in a race against time and circumstance. What could he do to prevent her from being thrown over the edge? The smaller dude straightened up and turned to look behind him. The ledge, made of solid rock, contained patches of loose gravel and he needed to exercise caution, lest he slipped and fell into the pit below.

The tall dude gave O'Malley a kick. The smaller dude turned to face Tam again and she looked up at him with beseeching eyes. He smiled.

"Don't do this," she croaked. Her mouth had dried up and her throat felt constricted. She heard a sound from a short distance away. It sounded like a rifle shot.

*

Conscious of the wind sheriff Cranwell lowered his eye to find the target and frame it in the scope. The wind blew straight off the mountain top into his face and with his eye narrowed to a mere slit he froze the image of his target into the center of the crosshairs. Even with the scope, the one-hundred and fifty-yard distance would be a difficult stretch for him. If he missed, Tam would be thrown over the ledge and O'Malley would follow. The two men would also open fire on him—cammo-dudes always carried firearms.

The image blurred as he tried to keep the target in the center of the crosshairs. He felt his eye tear up and with his heart pounding like a drum, he squeezed the trigger. The Remington bucked against his shoulder as the bullet flew toward its target. A fraction of a second later the dude flung both arms into the air as the projectile slammed into his chest. In a dramatic act of slow motion, the man toppled sideways and went down on the ledge. A chill flashed down Mortimer's spine—he had just killed a man. Without further thought, he swung the rifle to line up the second dude, who in stark surprise at his fallen comrade, froze to the spot.

The man overcame his shock and started to draw his weapon as Mortimer brought the Remington to bear. The dude managed to lift the revolver in an attempt to take aim, but the crack of the rifle resounded against the cliffs of the Groom Mountains. The sheriff lifted his eye off the scope's eyepiece. He saw the man's head jerk upwards and knees crumple under him as he fell over backward.

Sheriff Cranwell sprinted toward the ledge. He grabbed Tam's arm and pulled her away from the edge as the smaller dude's body toppled over into the void. The full realization of what happened hit him and he cradled his forehead in shaky hands. Tam lay on her side, in shock and sobs of relief started to rack her body. O'Malley's eyes bulged and then closed. A tear slid down his cheek and he started to choke. The sheriff jumped to his feet, rushed over to the agent and tore the gag from his mouth. O'Malley's breakfast followed and he puked it all up onto the ground.

Mortimer moved over to the taller dude and searched his trouser pocket for the cuff's keys. He found them and set the two agents free. O'Malley crawled over to Tam and took her in his arms. Their eyes filled with tears as they stared into each other's faces. He placed his forehead on her chest and they lay there in a tight embrace. There were no words to say.

After about five minutes the sheriff spoke for the first time. "That was a close call."

O'Malley lifted his head and stared at his savior. "How did you know?"

Tess at the hotel called me. I arrived to see the mayhem these two had caused and I realized something bad was afoot, so I followed. My brother and I used to play up here a lot when we were kids—I kind of knew where they were heading."

"You arrived in the nick of time, sheriff. A moment later and we would both have been dead. We owe you our lives," said Tam.

"It's nothing anyone else wouldn't have done under the same circumstances. When Tess called I realized my brother was wrong about you guys."

"Your brother?" asked O'Malley.

"Charles gets the impression you're on the side of the military and that I should not divulge anything regarding the town's position."

Tam gave him a wan smile. "We know the town's position, sheriff. We came to investigate something sinister at Area 51. It had to do with the death of the adjutant and the two missing scientists, but there appears to be so much more to the story."

The sheriff seemed relieved. "I thought you guys might be here because you suspected me and Charles of poisoning the town's people in order to blame the government for our woes."

Tam stood up to flex her stiff limbs. "The CIA has been monitoring this situation for a while, sheriff. We know your position regarding the government's desire to see Hemlock gone. We also know the military has been cooking something up. I am convinced the adjutant and the two scientists found out what was going on and they paid for it with their lives."

O'Malley also stretched out his limbs. "We should get back to the town. I need to contact our deputy director and give him a report. How's your leg, Tam?"

She rubbed her thigh and winced. "I'll be okay, but perhaps I should get that doctor at the field hospital to look at it. You did a great job, Dillon, but it needs to be cleaned again."

"We need to carry this big dude to my truck," said the sheriff. I'll have his body placed in the morgue at the field hospital. I also need to inform the base."

"What will you tell the military?" asked Tam.

"The truth, I guess. I am conflicted, however. If I tell them I shot him because he was about to murder you guys it will alert whoever is behind all this." said the sheriff.

"May I make a suggestion," asked O'Malley.

"Go on," said the sheriff.

"Tell them the dudes were up here on unknown business and you found this one, shot. You suspect the other fell over the edge. You can say you followed up on a distress call from Tess, at the hotel and you followed their four-by-four. Don't say anything else. I'll speak to Tess. Tam and I will take full responsibility for everything. My guess is they won't push you for more detail because they already know what the dudes were up to."

Sheriff Cranwell gave his suggestion some thought. "Okay. I'll do it. I want this whole thing sorted out so we can get our lives back. I'll hide the Remington in case someone comes looking for it."

"Good man," said O'Malley. "Let's get this dude down to your truck."

O'Malley and the sheriff lifted the dead man between them while Tam carried the rifle. They made slow progress back to the truck. Twenty minutes later they drove onto the sports field and parked in front of the marquee. O'Malley and the sheriff removed the dude's body and carried it around the marquee to the makeshift morgue, behind. Tam entered the tent to find Dr. Meyer.

She noticed the empty bed where her stricken contact, Sheila Graves, lay prior to their earlier departure. She stared at the crumpled bed linen. Dr. Meyer saw her and came over.

"She's gone—less than ten minutes ago. I'm sorry."

Tam nodded and choked up. O'Malley and the sheriff entered the marquee at the rear entrance and saw the two woman at the foot of the bed. O'-Malley placed his arm around Tam's shoulders.

"Do you think you could look at Miss Clyde-Walker's leg? She was shot earlier after we left here," he asked.

Dr. Meyer looked shocked. "I heard gunshots and I told Dr. Tobias—we couldn't figure out what had happened."

She turned to Tam. "Please have a seat and I'll take a look at your wound."

Tam still wore the shorts, pulled on in place of her torn jeans, after the black pickup incident. The doctor removed the bandage and examined the wound.

"It looks clean. I'll just get some antibiotic spray."

"Are you able to put weight on it?" asked O'-Malley.

She smiled. "I can if I can lean on you."

"You can lean on me all you want," said O'Malley. He leaned forward and kissed her on the lips. She placed her hands on each side of his face and reciprocated while the sheriff looked on with amusement. The doctor returned with the antibiotic spray in hand.

"You both look like you're getting cozy," she said.

They laughed. The doctor sprayed the wound and dressed it with a new bandage.

"That should do it. If you're still around in two days, pop in again and I'll check it," said Dr. Meyer.

The sheriff told her about the dude's body. "I will return and make out the necessary paperwork," he said.

Tam thanked the doctor and they left for the hotel. Tess sat at the front desk, busy on her computer when they walked into the reception.

"Oh, thank God you're both safe. Did the sheriff find you? Those two trouble makers caused a lot of damage in your room, Miss Clyde-Walker. I'll have to allocate you another one."

"Don't bother," said Tam. "We'll be staying in Special Agent O'Malley's room tonight."

Tess grinned. "I guess you two have grown a bit closer since I last saw you."

"You could say that," said O'Malley. The decision about the room appeared to be out of his hands.

"I guess you're both hungry. See you at 7:00 p.m.?" asked Tess

"We'll be there," said O'Malley.

Ж

# 18

## Back at the Hotel

After dinner O'Malley and Tam retired to their room. Tess and John, eager to know about their escapade, pushed for explanations but could glean little from the agents. When asked about the damage to the hotel and what should be done about it, O'Malley suggested they speak to the sheriff. He suggested they keep a low profile and not spread the word around.

Back in the room Tam removed her soiled clothes and stepped into the shower while O'Malley searched the scene of the attack in Tam's room. The gas, now dispersed through the broken sliding door and open windows, left a pungent smell. Tam's .38 and her phone lay untouched on the dresser. The glock, however, was nowhere to be seen, but after a quick search, he discovered it on the floor, beneath the bed.

Back in his room, O'Malley placed her pistol and phone on the dresser beside her. "They didn't take anything, but the room's a mess and smells awful."

"Those two thugs got what was coming to them. I guess there's no doubt as to who shot at us from the black pickup."

"According to John the pickup belongs to the scientist in charge of Hangar-3—Robin Clandecker," said O'Malley. "What are we going to do?"

Tam gave him a mischievous smile. "Go and shower, mister. There are more important things to do than worry about that right now."

O'Malley laughed. "I guess there are." He moved off to the bathroom, disrobed and stepped into the shower. The hot water ran over his head and down his body for a few minutes and he gave thought to what would happen when he returned to the bedroom. It occurred to him that he appeared to be the weak one in his marriage relationship. Women found him attractive and this placed a huge pressure on his resolve to be faithful in a relationship that lacked the vitality it once possessed. The memory of his daughter's death loomed like a hanging tree before him every time he thought of his marriage to Janet.

She made every effort to move on, but he could not overcome the grief. When he and Janet were together, Fallon's ghost always seemed to join them as a silent observer.

O'Malley pushed the thoughts from his mind. Tam's sudden intervention in his life served a selfish need and he could not think past the moment. He soaped himself and washed away the grime of the day. He exited the bathroom, slid onto the bed beside her and turned off the light.

\*

The early morning sunlight filtered through the curtains to wake O'Malley from a deep sleep. He felt confused when he raised his head to look around at the unfamiliar room. The events of the previous day came back with a rush of dread, but soon dispelled when he remembered the feel of Tam's soft body beneath his own.

He could hear the sound of the shower as steam, which billowed from the open bathroom entrance. He felt a strong urge to hold her strong, lithe body again and on an impulse, he threw the sheet aside and joined her in the shower.

Later in the morning, they sauntered down to the reception to find Tess.

"Looking for breakfast?" she asked. "I set up the poker table in the games room—just help yourselves."

They thanked her and moved to the games room, where they found breakfast cereal, milk, coffee, and toast. They both tucked in like ravenous beasts.

Tam's expression of contentment changed to that of concern as she thought about the future. "What are we going to do, Dillon?"

O'Malley swallowed a mouthful of cereal, then gave his answer. "I think we both need to contact our respective bosses first and make a report. I think you should go back to Vegas and rest that leg of yours."

Tam frowned. "I'm not leaving you for one minute, my love. Someone's got to keep you out of trouble."

He grinned at her. "You think I need you to deliver my ass from what's coming?"

"Tarzan needs a good, intelligent Jane at his side," she said.

He leaned back in his chair and laughed. "One who can't run away because of her sore leg?"

"Serious, Dillon. Don't think for a moment I'm incapacitated. We should both go back to Vegas and recoup, contact our superiors and see what they want us to do."

"I think that's probably a sensible thing. I believe we still have a part to play in flushing out the truth. My boss, James Ingram, might want to put someone else in to continue on the case, but I think we could just go back to the base as if nothing has happened."

"What do you mean?" she asked.

"Think about it. General Watkins already knows through the cammo-dudes failure to silence us, that we suspect the military of the adjutant's death. He'll realize that both the FBI and CIA know something's up and be too afraid to touch us."

"We'll have a target as big as the statue of Liberty on our backs if we do go back."

"All the better," said O'Malley. We know of three people who are definitely involved—Clandecker, Benson and the security guy, Blake. They all hang out at Hangar-3," said O'Malley.

Tam's eyes lit up. "I would love to get back into that place and check out what other secrets they're hiding."

O'Malley took out his phone and made a call.

"Sheriff? Do you think you can arrange some transport to get us back to Vegas?"

The phone conversation ended and O'Malley took a sip of his coffee.

"The sheriff will be here in thirty minutes, so we need to finish up. You should book yourself a hotel in Vegas. I already have one."

\*

The two agents settled their bills and said goodbye to John and Tess. They hugged their new-found friends and expressed appreciation for the meals and assistance rendered.

"It's more than likely we'll be back in the near future. Our business with Hemlock and the Military is not over yet," said Tam. She hugged Tess, who shed a few tears.

Sheriff Cranwell waited in the vehicle while the two agents completed their salutations.

They clambered in and waved a goodbye. "Ready to go?" he asked.

"I guess we are, Sheriff. How long will it take to Vegas?" asked O'Malley.

"It's an hour and a half's drive. What have you guys decided to do?"

"We'll report to our superiors and then return. My boss will have to have a strong conversation with General Watkins first, though."

"You're going to go back to the base after what's happened?" The sheriff sounded incredulous.

"We have no option. I doubt the military will try their luck a second time, now that they know we are aware of who tried to dispose of us."

"I see your point, Special Agent, but you will have to be extremely careful—as they say, accidents happen."

"Call me Dillon, Sheriff. Since you saved the two of us from ending up at the bottom of George's Pit, you can at least dispense with the formalities."

The sheriff chuckled. "In that case, please call me Morty."

"We'll always be eternally grateful for your intervention, Morty. Was that the first time you've had to kill someone," asked Tam.

The sheriff closed his eyes for a brief second. When he opened them Tam could see the reflection of pain. "It was the first time, and I can't stop thinking about it."

"It's never easy," said O'Malley. "I know you had no choice and we're sorry to have been the reason. "We are, however, eternally grateful for your intervention."

"I understand—I'll deal with it. Time takes care of all these things."

They drove on in silence, each consumed with their own thoughts. One hour and twenty minutes later they entered Vegas. O'Malley and Tam swapped phone numbers before the sheriff dropped them on the strip. They chose Tam's hotel first, a stone's throw from O'Malley's, and caught the elevator up to Tam's room. After a quick check around, they sat down on the bed and gazed into each other's eyes. O'Malley fell backward onto the bed pulling Tam down beside him. Their passion flared until Tam stood up abruptly. They embraced for several minutes until she rolled off and stood up.

"We need to contact our superiors and find out what they want us to do. Then, you must go back to your wife."

He sat up and blinked. "It's going to be hard being away from you."

Tam's shoulders drooped and she looked at her hands. "We really have to think about this relationship, Dillon. You have a teenage son and a wife who loves you. I'm on the rebound from my divorce and although you haven't talked about it, I can see you are still struggling with your daughter's death."

"That doesn't take away from the way I feel about you," he said.

"I know. I have very strong feelings for you, as well. All I'm saying is that we need to think about what's best for your son and where this relationship will take us."

He felt a sudden tension rise between them. "Were you always the sensible one in your family?"

This time she didn't laugh. "I'm being serious, Dillon. I'm deeply attracted to you, but we really need to think this through."

She turned to face the window. He got up off the bed and placed his arms around her. "We'll work it out," he said.

She turned to him and placed her forehead on his chest. "I want you so badly," she said. He pushed her chin upward and looked into her eyes. "We'll work it out, baby."

They held each other for a short while before he took her hand. "Let's pour ourselves a drink from the minibar and sit outside."

"Who is being the sensible one now?" she asked.

They poured the drinks and moved out onto the balcony where they made small talk and enjoyed one another's company for a short time.

He put down his empty glass. "I should go."

Tam pulled O'Malley to her and they kissed. She released him with reluctance as he turned, opened the door and looked back at her. Her eyes teared up and she rushed to him. He kissed her for the last time and pulled himself away.

O'Malley did not remember the ride down in the elevator but as he stepped out onto the sidewalk, outside the hotel reception, the hot air of Vegas hit him like a wall. He headed for his hotel and wondered if Janet would be there.

It had been two days since he left her and Steven, for Area 51. He felt guilty and conflicted about the sudden turn of events.

# 19

## Blake in trouble Again

General Watkins frowned at the man opposite him. Lieutenant Blake held his stare for a brief few seconds and then looked down at the floor.

"You're saying they escaped?" asked Watkins.

"It would appear so, Sir."

"Enlighten me how it is that I have placed my trust in your abilities to contain this growing mess and now it's going south?"

Blake looked up and caught the general's eyes. "I know I've failed you, Sir, but we will just have to deny sending the two dudes after O'Malley. I'll say they had some sort of vendetta against him and acted on their own."

"These are federal agents you are talking about, Lieutenant. They're not stupid. I'll now have both deputy directors on my case, thanks to your bungling."

I'm sorry, Sir. These were two of my best contractors and I never expected them to fail."

"Do you have any idea what happened?" asked the general.

"I received a call from one of the men to say the two agents were in their custody and were been taken out to George's Pit to be disposed of. Ten minutes ago I got a call from the sheriff of Hemlock, to say he discovered a cammo-dude's body on the ledge overlooking the Pit. The man had been shot. I asked him if he had seen the other dude, but he hadn't"

"Did you ask the sheriff what he was doing out there at George's Pit?"

"Said he was out hunting rabbits, Sir."

"It sounds a bit fishy to me," said the general. "What did he do with the body?"

"He took it to the field hospital and left it in their makeshift morgue."

"And there's no sign of the other dude?"

"Nothing, Sir. I suspect the agents overpowered both the dudes and perhaps the one fell into George's Pit—I just don't know."

"I'll have to get hold of Dr. Tobias. Maybe he can shed some light on this. I don't think the sheriff is telling us the whole truth."

"He could be holding something back, Sir. May I go?"

The general nodded and motioned toward the door with his hand. "Keep a lid on this. We'll make out as though nothing has changed. I'm sure O'-Malley and The CIA woman will think they'll be able to return without any incrimination. If they do, we'll set a trap for them."

*

O'Malley caught the elevator up to the seventh floor of the hotel and walked along the hallway to his room. He hoped Janet and Steven would still be out on the strip. It would give him time to relax a bit and call the deputy director.

He inserted his key card and opened the door. The bedrooms appeared to be empty and no sounds came from the bathroom or kitchenette. He went straight to the mini bar and poured himself a whiskey, with ice. A glance at his wristwatch confirmed there would be enough time to make a call to Washington D.C.

O'Malley placed the call and heard Ingram's deep southern drawl on the other end. They made small talk for twenty seconds before the deputy director asked for a report. O'Malley, in turn, asked if Ingram knew about the appointment of a CIA officer on the same case.

"It's just like the CIA," said Ingram. "They don't share important aspects of the work with us. As an intelligence group, they play their cards close to their chests. I will call my opposite number and make my frustration known."

O'Malley told him about the developments at the base and his thoughts on a possible conspiracy. He gave Ingram an excellent report on Tam and said he would work with her again, should she be up to it. He gave his opinion with regard to their continuance on the case as a team and shared his thoughts on their return to the base.

"I believe we'll be reasonably safe despite the conspirator's knowledge about our appointments. They will watch us but it would be difficult for them to harm us and hopefully, we will find out more."

The deputy director balked at first but then agreed with the premise.

"I will call General Watkins and tell him you went off to Hemlock on your own and needed to make a report to me regarding the status quo—that you will be returning to Area 51. Do you think he's involved?"

"I'm one hundred percent sure, Sir. I'll return to Area 51 tomorrow if you can get me on a Janet flight."

"I'll arrange it," said Ingram. "You look after yourself, Dillon."

O'Malley ended the call and relaxed on the king-sized bed. A moment later he fell fast asleep.

*

Janet O'Malley and her son Steven returned to the hotel after a full day on the strip. The hot, humid, air made her long for the air-conditioned room, supplemented with a cool drink. Her thoughts meandered toward her husband and she wondered how much longer he would be away. Steven missed his father and she wished matters were not so turbulent between her and her husband. Janet understood the grief and responsibility he felt for Fallon's death. Years of counsel by the FBI appointed psychologists, helped little.

At times he brooded over the matter at length and would disappear into his work, which did not help the relationship. Janet also knew the opposite sex found her husband attractive, which placed a pressure on her self-image. She loved her husband, but couldn't circumnavigate the mental barrier raised by the death of their daughter. It all seemed so unfair.

Mother and son caught the elevator up to the room in silence. Steven, a sensitive boy of seventeen did not understand the dynamics of his parent's relationship. He didn't resent his father but wished the family could move on. They never argued in his presence but he detected the tension. At times he hated his sister for dying.

Janet opened the door and walked into the room. She started at the sight of a man on the bed but realized it to be O'Malley.

"You're back." cried Steven. He stood at the foot of the bed and grinned at his dad.

O'Malley woke up as his wife leaned over to kiss his forehead. He smiled at them and sat up.

"Got in this morning, just before lunch."

"Is your job at Area 51 finished?" she asked.

"Unfortunately not. I have to go back tomorrow."

Steven's grin disappeared and he walked out of the bedroom.

"What's with him?" asked O'Malley.

"His disappointed you can't enjoy the vacation with us. He'll get over it. How much longer do you think you'll be?"

"A couple more days should do it. We can go out on the town tonight."

Janet did not seem enthusiastic. "I think both Steve and I are too tired. It's been so hot today."

"Okay," said O'Malley. We'll get dinner here in the hotel and spend the evening in the pool."

"Sounds good to me," she said.

Later the family entered the dining room and found a table. The dinner, buffet style, offered a wide range of foods and they all tucked in. While they were eating a woman walked in and took a table for two, on the opposite side of the room. O'Malley stared at her and to his consternation saw Tam, the last person he expected to see that evening. She flashed him a quick smile and then walked to the buffet counter.

He looked down at his food and try to compose himself. Janet saw the quick look and though she didn't see the smile from Tam, she did notice how uncomfortable her husband became after the woman's entrance.

"Is something wrong, Dillon? Do you know her?" Janet did not use an accusatory tone but tried to make it sound more like curiosity.

O'Malley cursed Tam's choice of his hotel as a dinner venue. He toyed with the idea that she came to spy on him out of curiosity, or maybe jealousy, but he didn't think she would be the type to do that.

"She works at Area 51—at the base."

Janet stared across the room at Tam who concentrated on her dinner and did not look up. "She's pretty. Is she a military employee?"

O'Malley considered telling a lie but realized it would be the worst thing he could do and decided, to tell the truth.

"She works for the CIA."

Janet nodded and continued with her meal, but shot an occasional glance at Tam. "Nice figure."

"O'Malley set down his knife and fork. "What's your point, Janet?"

"Nothing. I'm just asking you silly questions and making thoughtless comments." Her tone conveyed a slight but intended sarcasm.

He gave a single shake of his head and picked up the eating utensils.

Steven looked at his dad. "Do you actually work with her, dad?"

"No, not directly. The CIA is gathering intelligence at the base."

He felt a measure of guilt with the answer, and although not a lie, it skirted the truth. He did not once glance over at Tam, though he wanted to. His wife's sensitivity to the Agostino affair negated any hasty damage control he could do and he tried to think of how to put out the fire.

They concluded dinner with dessert and after a cup of coffee decided to leave the dining room. Tam's table stood close to the exit and O'Malley whispered in Janet's ear. "You and Steve go on—I'll catch up. It would be rude of me not to say hi to her."

Janet frosted over. "Of course, take your time." her answer bordered on sarcasm. O'Malley frowned at her and moved off toward Tam's table.

He stood and waited for Tam to look up from her dinner. She greeted him with a smile.

"Sorry to drop in you like this. I hope I haven't caused a problem."

He did not return the smile. "Tam—she's very perceptive and I couldn't hide my surprise. I think she suspects something."

"What did you tell her?"

"I told her that you work at the base but we don't work together."

I guess that was a wise move," said Tam.

"Did you come for a reason?" asked O'Malley.

"What better reason than I wanted to see you, however, I saw someone today whom we both know. I wanted to let you know in case it means something."

"Who are you talking about?" asked O'Malley.

"Robin Clandecker, from the base."

"Could just be a coincidence."

Tam stared into his eyes. "I miss you, Dillon."

He bowed his head. He wanted to hold her and make her pain disappear but instead, he stood there without a response. She leaned back in her chair.

"Clandecker's presence may be a coincidence, but it also may mean trouble."

"Did he see you?" asked O'Malley.

"No, but that doesn't mean anything. I gave my real name for the booking and it would be an easy matter for him to check the register."

"I guess so. What are you going to do?"

"I spoke to my boss. He wants me to go back if I feel safe enough to do so. The problem is they will know by now, that I work for the CIA. It could make things difficult for me."

"Perhaps you should consider not returning. Your injury also needs time to heal," said O'Malley.

"I wouldn't think of it. You'll need me there, and besides, I want to be with you."

"Okay, we'll meet at the Janet terminal tomorrow morning. I assume you're booked on the first flight to the base?"

"Yes, are you?"

"I don't know yet, but I suspect so. Ingram will let me know tonight," said O'Malley.

"I'll see you tomorrow then, my love," She stood in front of him. The scent of her entrapped him in a moment of wild panic—he wanted to kiss her, but he denied himself, stood back and allowed her to pass.

"Until tomorrow," he said with a distant look in his eyes.

She paid for her meal and left the hotel, while he returned to his room.

Janet sat on the couch with a vodka from the minibar. He tried to make a joke of the fact. "Getting drunk before bedtime?"

She gave him a hurt look. "I might as well. You're going off tomorrow morning and I don't know when I'll see you again. Perhaps your heart is there at the base."

"Jan..."

"Don't lie to me, Dillon. I saw the look that woman gave you. I thought it would be over after the Agostino woman—that you would learn there is no one who will ever love you like I do. But it seems I was mistaken."

O'Malley couldn't look her in the eye. His marriage-train hurtled toward destruction and he hated himself for it.

# 20

## Returning to Area 51

O'Malley and Tam met in the Terminal at 6:30 a.m. She sat alone with a magazine in one hand and a take-out coffee in the other. Earlier that morning he left the hotel before Janet woke up. He couldn't face another round with her and told her, before they retired to bed on the previous night, that she and Steven should head back to New York. He would follow on the completion of his mission.

Tam jumped up to meet him as he approached the gate. She set her coffee and magazine down on the ground, but in her haste, spilled the contents of the cup on the floor. O'Malley carried a backpack with one change of clothes and some toiletries with the hope the military had not stepped in and cleared out his dorm.

She flew into his arms and placed her forehead on his chest. They stood there for a long moment in a tight embrace, while the other passengers watched with amusement.

She looked expectantly up into his face. "It feels as though it's been ages since we were together."

"I feel the same," he reciprocated.

O'Malley still felt a little anger toward her with regard to the previous evening's dinner surprise, but he decided not to mention it. The sight of her turned him on. The smell and touch of her made him feel alive again and for the first time in a long while he felt happy. O'Malley loved the feel of her smooth skin and soft lips.

The gate opened, they presented their boarding passes and boarded the plane. Tam took the window seat and they fastened their safety belts as the Janet Jet's staff made preparations for takeoff. Once in the air, O'Malley relaxed.

"I assume you saw nothing more of Robin Clandecker?"

"Not exactly." She handed him a note. He took it and read:

STAY OUT OF HANGAR 3.

"Is this all?" asked O'Malley.

Tam nodded and took the note back. "They know we're returning and I assume that's because your boss called General Watkins."

"That just confirms our conclusions about Hangar-3. It may be a trap to bait us, but we have to figure out a way to get back in there," said O'-Malley.

"I think you might find your high-security clearance will have been revoked. Watkins won't allow you to snoop around at will."

O'Malley grinned. "I don't give a shit about the security clearance. I intend to go wherever I need to go."

She laughed. "That's what I expected you to say."

The twenty-minute flight ended with the pilot's announcement of their arrival at Area 51. After the aircraft rolled to a stop they made ready to disembark. O'Malley looked out of the window and saw a reception committee waiting for them.

He tapped Tam on the shoulder and pointed at the men. "That could be trouble."

Tam turned to look through the window. "I see Lieutenant Blake is at the head of it. At least they're not carrying firearms."

They walked down the stairs and stepped onto the runway. Lieutenant Blake appeared before them, with a crooked grin.

"Well, well. Just look at what flew in from gamble city."

"What can we do for you Lieutenant?" asked O'Malley.

"I have orders to immediately escort you to General Watkins. He is waiting."

"Talk to those two morons who arrested us, lately, Lieutenant?"

"I have no idea what you're talking about, O'-Malley. Just shut your trap and follow me."

Four men in cammo-uniforms fell in on either side of them as they walked toward the terminal. O'Malley glanced at his wristwatch—8:10 a.m. They left the terminal, marched past several buildings to the main headquarters and into the general's office reception area. Enid glared at them as the group stopped outside the base commander's door.

"Can the general see us now, Enid?" asked Lieutenant Blake.

Enid popped her head into the office and then motioned for them to enter. General Watkins sat like a tribal chieftain on his throne. O'Malley and Tam were not asked to sit down. "You can leave us, Lieutenant."

Blake saluted and left. The four-man security detail went with him.

The general eyed Tam and O'Malley out for a few seconds. "I understand you broke into Hangar-3, O'Malley."

I didn't break in General. Two of your men cuffed me and deposited me in a storeroom there. I had no idea it was a special area at the time."

"I don't buy into the story, O'Malley. I gave no such orders for you to be arrested."

"Then your men are acting without your knowledge, General."

"Your clearance does not extend to Hangar-3. If it were not for your boss, James Ingram, I would have you arrested and jailed for what you did. You got in via the air-duct system and obviously escaped the same way. I don't know what you think you saw there O'Malley but we will deny everything you say."

"I came at your request, General. I came to find out why your adjutant was murdered and what happened to those two scientists, not to break into your precious top secret area."

Watkins turned to Tam. "And you are Agent Clyde-Walker, with the CIA—not Maria MacDonald—the name you used to gain entrance to the base."

"You will have to speak to my superiors about why they wanted me here, General."

The general continued to eye them out. "I know why they sent you here, but you'll not find what you are looking for. Area 51 has always been a secret place and it will remain that way. Capitol Hill accepts that. I should chase your pretty ass off my base, Miss Clyde-Walker but instead, I won't rock the boat."

O'Malley interrupted. "We're only here, collectively, to find out what happened to the adjutant and those scientists, General. We are not interested in anything else."

"Then stay away from Hangar-3. It has nothing to do with the case you're working on."

"That suits us fine, General," said Tam. "We'll confine our search to the adjutant's death and those poor scientists, whom we believe discovered something so wrong that they paid for it with their lives."

"See that you do that, Miss Clyde-Walker." You're both to hand over your personal weapons to Edith—I will not permit you to carry firearms while on the base. You are dismissed—and only come back to bother me if you find anything pertaining to the death of my adjutant. I would like to have that resolved as quickly as possible."

They left the office without another word. O'-Malley removed the glock from its shoulder holster and Tam also removed her weapon. Edith took the two guns and locked them in a safe beneath her desk.

"You can pick these up from me before you leave the base," she said.

They left without comment and walked back toward the dorm area. "Your room or mine?" asked Tam.

"Let's use mine. I suggest we sit down and brainstorm how we're going to get back into Hangar-3."

*

They decided to have lunch at Sam's Place, a bar and fast food facility, which served light lunches and drinks for the base's not-so-hungry. The stroll past the baseball field took them fifteen minutes and on one side they could see the old water tower, with the new tower structure in the distant background. Straight ahead stood the DY-COMS radar building and further to the right, the older area which contained hangars four, five, six and seven. Sandwiches and coffee were delivered out on the bar deck.

"Any ideas as to what we can do to get into Hangar-3," asked Tam.

O'Malley took a bite of his sandwich and contemplated the possibilities.

"We need to find someone who works in there on a regular basis. One thing we can be sure of—the vent system will be closed off to entry from outside. If we're to get inside it will have to be through the main entrance."

"The entrance's electronic system will be difficult to override. You're intimating we need someone to sneak us through in a vehicle?" asked Tam.

"It's the only idea I can come up with at the moment. I still have a flash drive with a list of all the base's personnel and where they work. I'm surprised the general didn't ask me to return it."

Tam took a sip of her coffee. "I can get the CIA to look into the backgrounds of any of those whom we single out."

O'Malley became conscious of two people who walked out onto the deck to sit down at a table near them. He glanced over Tam's shoulder in the direction of the two and frowned.

'What's up," asked Tam.

"Captain Benson and Robin Clandecker have just sat down at a table behind you. Clandecker is staring in our direction."

"Oh shit," said Tam. "I hope we're not going to have a confrontation."

"I would think that unlikely," said O'Malley.

They ate on in silence, conscious of the men's scrutiny. After another ten minutes of small talk, they finished their lunches and drained the last drops of coffee.

"Let's go," said O'Malley. They stood and walked toward the deck steps on the east of Sam's place, which looked out toward the old hangar area. As they reached the stairs, Captain Benson shouted from his table.

"Stay away from our high-security areas."

O'Malley stopped in his tracks and turned to face the two men, who remained seated at their table. "I have the necessary clearance to visit any area I need to."

Clandecker grinned. "Everywhere but one place, O'Malley—Hangar-3."

O'Malley hesitated for a moment. "And what is it exactly that you don't want us to see in Hanger-3?"

"I believe you already know something about it. You've snooped around there once before," said Benson.

O'Malley turned to Tam. "Let's get out of here. I find a certain smell is putting me off."

They turned, walked down the stairs and out in the direction of their dorm. The two men stared at them for a long while and when they were out of earshot, Clandecker turned to Benson. "Make sure Blake keeps a good eye on those two scabs."

"He will. You can be sure they'll try to break in and enter the lower levels."

"If that happens we need to be ready for them," said Clandecker. "Make sure the gate's electronics cannot be compromised."

The two agents walked back to the dorm, where O'Malley opened the safe and removed the flash drive. He inserted it into his laptop and Tam leaned over his shoulder to view the contents. He scrolled down the lists of names until he reached the top secret section.

Hangar-3, with Clandecker as supervisor, appeared with a list of seven people who worked under him. "Make a note of these names," said O'-Malley.

Tam grabbed the pad and pen supplied by courtesy of the military and began to write down the names he called out.

"The name of Dr. Bannister can be removed. I believe he's lying at the bottom of George's Pit, may he rest in peace," said Tam.

"How will you get the details to your office in D.C.?"

"I know one of the pilots. He is on the CIA's payroll—another contractor," she said.

He grinned and took her hand. "I have an urgent need."

She gave him a sultry smile and they headed for the bed.

Ж

# 21

## O'Malley's Discovery

The detailed analysis report of the names on Hangar-3's project would arrive the next morning with the pilot of the Janet jet. In the meantime, Tam returned to her office in the main administration building and left O'Malley to work on further events which pertained to the death of Adjutant Greenberg. O'Malley walked over to Greenberg's office. On the unlocked door hung a sign, which designated it as "off-limits" to unauthorized personnel. He wondered if evidence might have been missed in his initial search and he opened the door to peek inside. There appeared to be no disturbance of items on the desk, but a quick search for the journal confirmed its removal.

O'Malley stepped over to the bookcase for a quick look through the book titles.

On the second shelf from the top, a book which appeared to have a fractured spine caught his eye. The book's name appeared a little obscure because of the fracture and to read it he pulled the book off the shelf. The name of the book, "Travels into Several Remote Nations of the World," a book well known to him, explored the travels of Lemuel Gulliver, who took a trip to Lilliput with its tiny citizens. The writing always struck O'Malley as one of the greatest satires on human nature. As he removed it from the shelf a thin sheet of folded paper, fell out onto the floor.

Intrigued, he bent down to pick it up to have a look at the contents. The folded piece appeared to be the old DOT-MATRIX printer paper, with holes on either side in continuous form and about eighteen inches long. He opened it and saw a ninety percent redaction job on the type. O'Malley glanced at the heading and saw:

E.M. Technologies.

Evaluation of Nano Technology, Operation Omega.

Dr. P.T. Nelson.

Dept. of Nano-robotics.

Two names jumped out at him. He recalled the name of the company, "E.M. Technologies," on a document in the Hanger-3 office filing cabinet after his escape from the storeroom. The name of Dr.

P.T. Nelson struck a bell but he couldn't quite place it. He decided to inspect the full contents later. He returned the book to the shelf, folded the paper and slipped it into the pocket of his windbreaker. The rest of the books revealed little else of importance, so he left the office and returned to his room.

The name, P.T Nelson, still bothered him as he sat down at the narrow desk and opened his laptop. He Googled E.M. Technologies and discovered that the company worked with nanorobotic applications. Several nano-healing systems were under scrutiny by the medical fraternity, of which two claimed to be potential breakthroughs. One of the systems pertained to internal organ reparations. The article's report of "miracles" achieved by the company since their rise to fame in 1998, caught his eye. An obscure article on the second page of his search sent a chill down his spine:

"E.M. Technologies signs contract with Military."

The article, dated March 2015 gave no details of the contract's specifics, but the name of Dr. P.T. Nelson featured with some prominence. He would be responsible for a nano laboratory in an "obscure location".

O'Malley knew where that obscure location was situated: Area 51. He removed the flash drive from the safe and inserted it into the USB port. A quick scan of the departments produced a section under Robin Clandecker's Hangar-3 top secret operation, referred to as the "Lab". The first name which appeared there belonged to E.M. Technologies scientist, Peter Nelson.

He returned to the Google search and keyed in the name. A result came up and the first one at the top of the page, caught his eye:

*Prominent Scientist Listed as Missing.*

*Peter Nelson, a representative of E.M Technologies of Seattle, Washington, has been reported missing from his hotel room in Las Vegas. Dr. Nelson, on a weekend break from his job at the Area 51 base, was last seen with a colleague, Dr. George Bannister, who has also been reported as missing, almost two weeks ago....*

O'Malley sat back in his chair and looked up at the ceiling. A faint smile played on the corners of his mouth as he began to understand the dynamics of what appeared to be a conspiracy. The two missing scientists, on the discovery of an illegal project, tried to warn the adjutant, and it cost them their lives.

Robin Clandecker appeared to have close involvement with this program, and it appeared to be exclusive to everyone, but a few. Other important players would be Captain Benson and General Watkins. Lieutenant Blake of Security also played a role, but perhaps did not know the full extent of the heinous scheme and its consequences for the town of Hemlock.

He couldn't wait to tell Tam. He pulled the folded matrix-paper from his pocket and opened it.

Apart from a few obscure words and three sentences, almost the entire contents of the document could not be read because of the redaction. The penciled circles contained single words, each followed by a question mark. Greenberg must have received the redacted document with its pencil notations, from one of the missing scientists.

Several of the notations referred to "scaled down parameters" with question marks in pencil, alongside them.

A notation of, "failure guaranteed", penciled above another redacted sentence drew his attention.

The door opened to break his intense concentration and Tam entered the room.

"The head of materials, a stupid and extremely rude major, wanted to fire me because I was absent without consent for the last two days."

"What did you say?" asked O'Malley.

"She laughed. Since my cover is actually blown I decided to have some fun. I produced my badge and told him I had been sent to watch him."

O'Malley's eyes lit up. "And?"

"He went all colors and almost had a heart attack. He started to curse the general and said that Watkins had never had any time for him—that he would have been a colonel by now but for the general."

"I guess he became quite friendly after that?"

"He practically fawned at my feet," said Tam. "Did you discover anything more in Greenberg's office?"

O'Malley told her about the sheet of matrix paper, stuck away in Gulliver's travels. He went on to relate what the Google search revealed about E.M Technologies.

"I believe I know what's going on," he said.

"Enlighten me, my darling," she said.

"I think the two scientists discovered the real motivation for the project being run by Robin Clandecker. Dr. Peter Nelson was a lead scientist for the E.M Technologies research team in the final decade of the last century until he came over to work on a military application for nanorobotics in 2015."

He opened the matrix paper and continued his explanation. "Look at the heading on this brief. It's from the department of nano-robotics and makes reference to self-eradication technology. What do you think that means?"

Tam squinted at the paper. "I'm not a scientist but I would say it's talking about nano-robotics being developed for medical purposes."

O'Malley concurred. "Do you remember when we spoke to Dr. Tobias at the field hospital? We were speaking about the water supply and the possibilities of it having been poisoned—he appeared a bit defensive about the water having been tested and the reference to a residue—that it was not conclusive. What if Clandecker has been working on a new technology to do with self-eradicating robotics? The product disappears after a while, leaving no trace of its original presence. What if they are using these tiny robots to cause the organ failure?"

Tam raised her eyebrows as the possible answer to the mystery at Hemlock began to surface in her mind. "You are saying that the military had engineered a nano-robot that causes massive organ failure and self-eradicates its presence in the water supply after a short time?"

"You must have read my thoughts, sweetheart," answered O'Malley.

"Look at the notation someone has made here." He pointed to a circled notation above a redacted sentence on the matrix paper.

Tam read it out allowed. "Failure guaranteed. They could be referring to internal organs."

"Exactly," said O'Malley. A smile of triumph adorned his face.

"The scientists who worked on it initially didn't realize what it would be used for," said Tam.

O'Malley elaborated on her thoughts. "When they finally realized that nanorobots would be used to kill people and not heal them, they decided to pull the plug and told Greenberg."

"It makes perfect sense when you put it like that—you should be working for the CIA, my love," said Tam.

"Perfectly happy with the FBI, thanks," returned O'Malley. He grabbed her by the arms and swung her around onto his lap. They hugged and kissed for a while until Tam shook free of his grasp.

"Come on Special Agent O'Malley, we've got work to do. I must get the details of that list to the pilot when he arrives from Vegas. They don't stay on the base for longer than an hour—it's a turnaround flight. We need that analysis as soon as we can get it."

They left the dorm and walked to the Janet Terminal where the ground crew was busy with a check of the aircraft's vitals.

"I know where the pilots will be. Follow me," said Tam.

O'Malley grabbed her arm. "I noticed two cammo's started to follow us when we left the dorm. They're behind us right now."

Tam looked a bit perplexed. "I don't want them to see me talking to the pilot. Can you waylay them while I slip away?"

"I'd love to," said O'Malley. He turned and walked straight toward the two men, who eyed him nervously.

"Can either of you tell me the time?" he asked.

The men looked taken aback with the sudden distraction and he saw one of them search out the area ahead to look for Tam. "If you're looking for the lady she's just slipped into the washroom."

The one dude reacted angrily. "We don't know what you're talking about, mister."

"Oh, I see. Okay—don't worry about it." he walked off and left them.

O'Malley moved over to the concession and purchased two coffees for takeout. Five minutes later Tam appeared with a satisfied smile on her face.

"It's done. He says we should get the answer back by tomorrow morning when he returns with the jet."

Great work, love," said O'Malley. He handed over the cup of coffee and they left the terminal.

"Let's go and get ready for dinner," he said.

"That's a great idea, but I have something just as delectable to suggest before we eat."

He laughed and swung his arm over her shoulders.

*

Later that evening, after dinner O'Malley and Tam decided to pay her friend, Henry, a visit. They were concerned that the general might have worked out who helped them get off the base without detection. A few knocks brought Henry to the door.
"Come on in," he said.

Tam sat down on the bed and O'Malley in the single chair, provided for the room. Henry sat on the carpet with his legs folded beneath him. He wore a concerned look on his face.

He addressed Tam. "I was asked a whole lot of questions by that Lieutenant Blake the day following your escape, off the base. I was surprised to see you back at work this afternoon and wanted to talk, but the boss seemed a bit steamed up about something."

"We just wanted to make sure you were okay," said Tam.

"I answered all their questions and flatly denied helping you. Was your stay at Hemlock successful?"

"Very successful," answered O'Malley. "Have you ever been into Hangar-3, Henry?"

He looked at O'Malley with incredulity. "That's a highly restricted area—only people with top secret clearances can go in. I believe it has three levels."

"Three?" asked Tam. "I thought it was only two levels."

"That's what you see on all the base's maps. It only shows levels one and two officially, but I have it on good authority from a friend, that a third level preceded the first two by several years. The first and second came much later and were built on top of the original level."

"They must have planned that a long time ago," said O'Malley.

"My friend told me it was all planned in the eighties. He worked for the contractor who built the entire bunker."

"This friend of yours—do you still have contact with him?" Tam asked.

"We talk on occasion. He likes to hear what's happening with things here; lives in Vegas."

"We would love to talk with him if that would be at all possible," said O'Malley.

"I don't know, but I can ask," replied Henry.

Ж

# 22

## Searching for an Ally

After a restless night, both Tam and O'Malley went their respective ways after breakfast. Tam asked O'Malley to meet with the pilot of the Janet jet and pick up the employee analysis files on Hangar-3's personnel.

"I told him you and I were working together and that he would find you in the men's washroom—just show your badge for identification purposes. It will give me time to catch up on my admin work."

O'Malley made his way to the terminal and waited for the jet to arrive. He checked to make sure no one would see him slip into the washroom. A few minutes later the pilot sauntered in walked up to the urinal. O'Malley flashed his badge.

The pilot nodded and handed him a flash drive. "They said to check out the details on a Dr. Paul Shaw—he may be the man you're looking for. Destroy the drive when you are finished."

O'Malley thanked him and left. Back in the dorm room, he checked out the files. Robin Clandecker came up first. A graduate of the Clear Lake University in Houston, Texas, followed by the completion of a Master's and Doctorate in Seattle, Washington, Clandecker set his sights on a career in nanotechnology. Clandecker worked for several companies before he landed a lead role in nanotechnology, with E.M Technologies, in 2002. He then moved on to work for the Military as a civilian contractor, and in 2008, took over the supervision of a top secret project.

O'Malley scanned through several of the other employees until he came across Paul Shaw's file. Shaw graduated from a university in Colorado where he also completed Master's and Doctorate degrees, with majors in nano-technology. He became a civilian contractor with the military in 2013, after five years of employment with the Wyss Institute at Harvard University. The institute specialized in folded DNA segments used for 3d structures.

Shaw's service provided an important clue to the military's intended direction with their nano research. One of the aims of DNA origami, the use of nanobots to attack tumors, would be crucial to the end result of the secret project and he brought an expertise to the table which complimented this development.

O'Malley's interest peaked, however, when Shaw's record showed his many arguments with Clandecker, who wanted to fire him, but General Watkins refused. It would appear that Shaw did not trust Clandecker and his intended direction for DNA origami.

O'Malley met with Tam at Sam's Place for lunch and could not contain his enthusiasm for the discovery.

"I think I've found just the right person to help us in our quest to break this whole thing wide open."

Tam listened while she ate her sandwich. "Hangar-3's staff work on a shift basis which alternates between twelve hour days and nights. They all stay in the same dorm which is down near the old toxic-waste, burning pits."

"We need to pay him a visit, soon," said O'Malley. "I would like to speak with Henry's friend first. We need to establish if there isn't an Achilles heel to the bunker's set up."

"Henry will let us know later this evening. How to achieve such a meeting will be the real question, though."

"One of us will have to fly back to Vegas to meet him,"

Tam placed her hand on his. "It will have to be you, sweetheart. You have the higher clearance level, which kind of suggests a seniority. The general doesn't appear to be worried what you do, as long as you stay out of Hangar-3."

"Well, let's not count our chickens before they hatch. Henry's friend still has to agree to talk."

"I think when he finds out you're FBI, he'll open up."

They chatted for a while, finished their coffees and walked back to Tam's office where O'Malley left her and headed for an hour in the gym. Later he returned to the dorm where he bumped into Henry.

"Just the person I want to see," said Henry.

"What's up," asked O'Malley.

"I'm taking a drive over to Hemlock to talk to the supermarket owner. We seemed to have received some grocery products that should have gone to them. Normally I would have sent them back to the supplier but it seems a good opportunity to call my friend who worked on the bunker."

"Sounds good to me. I understand all calls from the base are monitored, so that's an excellent idea."

"I'll be leaving in fifteen minutes. I'll meet you outside my office—you know which vehicle I use for my travels."

"Could you quietly let Tam know I'm going with you?"

"Will do. I know you both work for law enforcement—are you two an item?"

"Sort of," said O'Malley. "Let's just say we are close working colleagues."

He knew Henry fancied Tam so he didn't want to get into a conversation about his real relationship with her. Henry raised his eyebrows. "Close working colleagues, eh? I wouldn't mind being in that position with her."

O'Malley grinned. "You work in the same office block. You could say you have a close working relationship."

"Not close enough," he smiled. "See you in a short while."

*

Henry dropped O'Malley outside the sheriff's office while he sorted out his business with the supermarket and made a call to his friend.

"I'll only be about thirty minutes," he said.

"Take as much time as you need, Henry. I see the sheriff's pickup, so I'll be here when you return."

O'Malley opened the office door and found the sheriff at work. "Too busy to see an old friend?" asked O'Malley.

The sheriff grinned and leaned back in his chair. "What brings you to Hemlock, Dillon?"

"Just came to see if I could cause you some more excitement. How are things in the town?"

Mortimer motioned him to the chair on the opposite side of his desk. "We haven't had any further deaths, nor have I heard any strange vehicles traveling through town in the early hours of the morning. All is quiet on the western front."

"Have you heard from Dr. Tobias regarding further tests on the water?"

'They don't appear to have made any further headway," said the sheriff.

O'Malley shifted in his seat. "I think Tam and I have discovered what the possible cause may be, however, we still have to find proof."

"I assume you and Tam are back at Area 51? What is it you've discovered?"

"This must remain between us for the moment," said O'Malley. "We believe the military, or someone at the base, is doing experimentation with nano-robotic technology. It's possible that your water supply might have been compromised with a product they have produced."

The sheriff's eyes opened wide. "—and my guess is they must have invented some sort of robot which will attack the internal organs of human beings?"

'That's our theory. For this to happen means they have found a way to make the evidence disappear," said O'Malley.

"Christ. It's a bit of a stretch to think the military would poison the people of Hemlock, but anything's possible—especially when I consider what they intended to do to you and Tam."

"They probably needed a small group on which to experiment, and given the history, I think the town would have seemed the ideal proposition," said O'Malley.

The sheriff gazed with thoughtful contemplation out of the window. He ran his hand through his hair. "It makes sense. Charles will be extremely interested to hear about this."

"I would appreciate it if you didn't say anything to your brother just yet. We need more proof. I have a feeling there is much more to this than just the poisoning of Hemlock's water."

"As you wish, Dillon, but Charles has just as much need to hear this as I did."

"I know, Morty, however, the fewer people there are in the loop at this point, the better. I will take a walk down to the field hospital. Is Tobias still there?"

"No. He left for Las Vegas last night. Dr. Meyer is there, though."

"I'll give it a miss for now," said O'Malley.

A honk on a horn from a vehicle outside the station advised O'Malley of Henry's return.

"I have to go. Look after yourself and if you see Tess and John, tell them I said hi."

Sheriff Cranwell stood and walked around the desk to shake O'Malley's hand.

"Look after yourself, Dillon. You're in a place of danger."

"Thanks, Morty. I'll be in touch. It was good to see you again."

O'Malley left the office and climbed into Henry's vehicle. "Successful?" he asked.

Henry grinned. "You owe me a couple of beers. I spoke to Clem and told him you would be willing to come to Vegas tonight on the Janet transporter—I hope it's not too soon for you."

"Tonight's fine," said O'Malley. You'll have to move it to get back to the base so I can catch the jet."

"Hold onto your hat, Special Agent."

Henry pushed the gas pedal to the floor and the eight-cylinder SUV responded with a throaty roar.

*

O'Malley said goodbye to Tam and walked out onto the runway, toward the mobile stairway. In consideration of the time constraint, he discouraged her attempt to accompany him on the flight. Apart from meeting with Clem Harris, Henry's friend, he also needed to drop in on Janet as they would leave for Newyork in the morning. He also wanted to arrange to spend time with Janet to discuss their future on his return to Newyork. He needed to talk to his son and confirm his ongoing support and love.

The flight to Vegas gave him a little time to think things through with regards to his marriage. He wanted to end the continuous loop of discontentment—they both needed a new start. He loved Tam; they belonged together. Janet would be better off if she found someone whom she deserved. He meant that in the best possible way. She did not need someone stuck in a time-warp of depression, because of a daughter's death. Life with Janet involved a constant reminder of Fallon.

His meeting with Clem Harris arranged for 9:00 p.m. gave him a few hours to spend with his wife and son. He intended to surprise her and just hoped she would agree to see him. If she wouldn't talk to him he would at least be able to speak to his son.

On arrival at Vegas airport O'Malley made his way to the hotel, but before going up to the room, he decided to stop in at the bar and fortify himself with a drink. He ordered and sat at the bar counter to settle his mind. Two whiskey's and thirty-five minutes later he plucked up the courage and left the bar for the elevator. He felt the effect of the alcohol hit home as he stepped out of the elevator and headed toward the suite. His mind relaxed and he knocked on the door.

Steven opened the door and gave a gasp in surprise. "Dad. I didn't expect to see you for a while."

O'Malley smiled and gave his son a hug. "I wanted to see you before you and your mom left Vegas," he said.

Janet remained on the settee, her face expressionless. O'Malley felt a little self-conscious.

"Hi, Jan..."

She looked at her son. "Steve, please go to you room—your father and I have something to discuss."

"I'll come and talk to you when we're finished, buddy," said O'Malley.

Steven frowned at his mother and stalked off to his room. O'Malley sat down opposite Janet and waited for her to speak.

"I don't think there is much I can say, Dillon. You've made your mind up to end our relationship and quite honestly, I think it will be the best thing for us."

O'Malley reeled at her direct approach. "You don't want to talk about it? I would like to settle things with you, Jan..."

"There isn't anything to settle. You can see your son whenever you need to—I'll not come between him and you. I will see a lawyer when I return tomorrow and start proceedings."

"I see," said O'Malley. "Then I'll just say good-bye to Steve." He stood and walked to his son's room.

"Hi, buddy. I hope you'll be able to forgive me for this but it looks like it's going to be a permanent arrangement this time."

He embraced his son and held him for several seconds. Steven pushed him away. "Don't sweat it, dad. I understand. Mom and I are just not good enough for you."

"It's not like that at all, Steve. You're my son and I'll always love you. It is I who am not good enough for you—I don't deserve you, but I will do everything I can to make things up to you."

Steven vented his anger. "You can't make up for all your absenteeism, or for what you've done to mom. I know you love me, dad, but you have a strange way of showing it. Please, just leave me alone. We'll go back home and get on with our lives."

"Steve...listen to me, please..."

"Please go, dad. I can't talk about it now. I want to be left alone."

O'Malley's heart felt as though it would fail him. He dropped his head and backed out of the room. Steven threw himself onto the bed and covered his head with the pillow.

"Now, you can see what your destructive lifestyle has done to your family. We not only lost our daughter but we've lost each other. You've alienated your son—I hope your latest adventure was worth it." Janet dropped her face into her hands and started to sob.

"Jan, please..." stammered O'Malley.

"Just go. Go back to that woman and leave us alone," shouted Janet.

O'Malley turned and walked to the door. He felt as though his heart would break and his world started to unravel. When he hit the cooler evening air he remembered the real reason why he came back to Vegas. He started to walk off in the direction of the bar where he would meet with Clem Harris.

# 23

## The Palm Palace Bar

The Palm Palace bar, situated in one of the side streets off the strip, provided a quiet atmosphere with soft music. It gave O'Malley the momentary impression of time-travel back to the fifties. The front end of an old Cadillac classic, built into the wall above the bar, dominated the area above and behind the bar counter. An old jukebox delivered Bennie Goodman music plus the velvety voice of Nat King Cole to a handful of listeners. Maybe Clem Harris chose the place because of the low-intensity lighting or for the music, but it served the intended purpose of their meeting

O'Malley took a booth on the right-hand side at the rear of the pub. He ordered a beer from an attractive waitress who gave him the eye and lingered long after he paid her for the drink. He thanked her and parted with a five dollar tip, which she stuck into her bra. He looked around and saw two other people in separate booths by themselves.

A minute later a tall man strolled toward him with a beer in hand. The man spotted O'Malley and walked toward the booth with a slow dip of his chin in acknowledgment.

"Special Agent, O'Malley?"

"You must be Clem," said O'Malley.

The man's smile revealed dimples on either side of his face, beneath high cheekbones and the slight slant to his eyes suggested an Asian origin. He sat down on the bench opposite and set his beer down in front of him.

"Henry told me a little bit about what you are looking for. I signed a non-disclosure agreement with the military about this stuff, but I figured you as being FBI I would consent to speak about my experience. I brought something for you."

He reached into the inside pocket of his coat, pulled out a folded piece of paper and opened it for O'Malley to see the sketches.

O'Malley craned his neck forward and squinted at the drawing in front of him.  Rough pencil diagrams showed the floor plans of three levels, with cross sections.

"I recognize this floor plan. I was in there for a short while." He pointed to the plan of the top floor, level one.

Clem took a sip of his drink and tapped his finger on a few spots. These are the other three floors. Very few people know about the bottom floor, even though it was built first, in the early eighties. All the base drawings of the bunker that exist at Area 51 show only the top two floors."

"Do you know the reason why they don't show it?" asked O'Malley.

"The word amongst the few that knew of it, say it became a storage for alien artifacts, maybe even an alien craft. It's just a rumor but you never know."

"I know there's a laboratory on the first floor and something definitely strange on the second level, below," said O'Malley.

"I don't know what changes might have been brought about but I guess you're looking for a way in?" Clem raised his one eyebrow.

"We managed to get in and out via the air vent system but that will be closed off to us now."

Harris took out a pen from his top jacket pocket and began to make dotted lines on the floor plan of the third level. "Here's something only a few know about. It's a floor drain, designed to take a reasonable volume of water, which I assumed would be a part of some future requirement. The drain is big enough to take a man crawling on his hands and knees. It's built of reinforced concrete and extends from the bunker out to a holding tank, also made of concrete. There is a kind of a gooseneck over here." He drew a box-like square on the sketch to indicate the position.

"What's the goose-neck for?" asked O'Malley.

"This will be the most difficult part of a breaking in. The goose-neck opens out into a catchment pit and both are filled permanently with water. As water runs down this drain from the floor, it causes the water to flow into the gooseneck and over a weir, into the catchment pit—just like a huge toilet. The water is pumped out of the pit, up to the ground's surface and into a French drain. There is a submersible pump in the catchment pit which keeps the water level in the pit and gooseneck at a constant level."

"Is there a cover over the pit?"

"A steel grid—nothing that can't be handled by two people."

O'Malley stared at the diagrams and sucked on his beer. "How long is the drain?"

"About thirty yards from the halfway point of the basement to its outer wall, and another fifty yards to the pit."

"This is exactly what we need. What do I owe you for this information?"

Clem laughed. "Perhaps we can meet at another time and you can tell me what the hell Area 51 has been hiding all these years."

"Depends on its classification." They both chuckled.

"I thank you for this Clem. You can rest assured you have done the citizens of America a good deed."

They drained their beers and O'Malley stood to leave.

"Give Henry my best," said Clem. O'Malley raised his finger to his forehead in a mock salute. "You bet. Look after yourself and thanks again for meeting with me."

With earlier hopes for a return to the hotel dashed by Janet's reception, he needed to find alternate accommodation for the night. A brief consideration of hotels crossed his mind, but thoughts of Tam soon took over and he longed for her company. Twenty yards behind two figures appeared out of the darkness and appeared to follow him. For a moment panic seized his normal self-confidence. The glock still lay in a safe in Edith's office. O'Malley quickened his pace and the followers reciprocated. He needed to get out of the side street and onto Vegas Boulevard, amongst the people and the bright lights.

He tried to remember if anyone might have entered while he and Clem were discussing business. He could not recall anyone following him out of the pub when he left. These two characters appeared out of the night, like ghosts. They were both very tall men, dressed in long, dark overcoats with the collars turned up and wide-brimmed hats. He wondered if they weren't perhaps actors from a movie set or stage production. O'Malley lengthened his stride and cast a nervous glance over his shoulder. To his surprise, the men appeared much closer than he thought them to be, and with long strides of their own they pulled up alongside him, one on each side.

O'Malley didn't panic. "What do you guys want? I don't have any money."

"We're not after your money, Special Agent O'Malley. We are here to warn you about your intentions at Area 51." The voice sounded deep and almost digitized.

O'Malley slowed down and stopped. The two men appeared to glide to a halt beside him and he tried to see their faces, but the street light lacked sufficient illumination. The collars of their overcoats cast deep shadows over their features. Long unkempt hair showed beneath their hats and they both appeared to have half-masks which covered their lower faces.

"Who are you and how do you know I work at Area 51?"

"Let's just say we have a vested interest in what you're trying to achieve there," said the one stranger. "We know about your meeting this evening and what you and Clem Harris discussed."

O'Malley wondered if he was dreaming. "Did General Watkins send you?"

"General Watkins did not send us, but Maguilor did."

"Who is Maguilor?" asked O'Malley. The name sounded familiar but he couldn't place it.

"It doesn't matter for now. We want to warn you not to use the drain, to enter Hangar-3."

"How do you know all this?" O'Malley's incredulity had increased a hundred fold. "How do you know about my discussion with Clem Harris?"

"Let's say we have an unfair advantage over you, Special Agent."

The man's tone remained non-threatening. "Just do not use the drain. Clem Harris is not who he pretends to be."

"What do you mean? Who is Harris, then?"

"He is not your friend. If you use his entry method you will be killed."

O'Malley peered at the man to ascertain more detail but the shadows prevented any compound definition. He leaned in for a closer look and managed to make out a pair of large eyes that seemed abnormally wide apart. The agent narrowed his own eyes in order to focus and noticed the bulges at the temples. A strange sensation of paralysis gripped him—the effect could have been psychological. His mind, however, remained on the alert throughout the entire confrontation.

"If you know so much about what's going on what do you suggest I do—how else can I gain entrance to the bunker?"

The conversation took a sudden turn toward a spirit of mutual cooperation.

"We warn you, Special Agent O'Malley, your efforts will be resisted by military command with everything they have at their disposal. There are things afoot over which you have no possible control. I will say this one thing, however—you can trust Paul Shaw."

O'Malley's jaw dropped. "You know about Paul Shaw?"

"We know everything, Special Agent, but there is little we can do. We have no power granted us in this situation."

"Power granted by whom?"

"We have said enough. I will warn you once more: do not use Hangar-3's drain. You will be throwing your life away."

The two men turned and walked off in the opposite direction. The murkiness of the night swallowed the strangers and left O'Malley in a state of wonderment. His body shook all over as he contemplated the strangest meeting he had ever experienced. One name stuck in his mind—Maguilor. The name struck a chord in his memory, but he could not remember why.

After a few minutes, his body started to cooperate again and he walked on toward the strip. The lights became brighter as he drew nearer to Las Vegas Boulevard. He wondered where he should seek shelter for the night. The hotel of Tam's recent stay came to mind and he decided to make his way there. The receptionist glanced at the register.

"I'm afraid we are full, sir. Why don't you try the Grand Chateau on East Harmon Avenue?"

He thanked her and returned to Vegas Boulevard to walk the four blocks to where East Harmon crossed the main street. Half an hour later he found the Grand Chateau, booked a room and opened the minibar, which held a variety of alcoholic beverages. O'Malley poured himself a Red Label and slumped down on the bed to reflect on the meeting with the strange men. He wondered what made him think the men seemed so unearthly and shook his head several times with vigor when the thought of alien beings settled in his mind

"Not possible," he mumbled. He finished the whiskey and returned to the bar for a second. After three more miniature bottles of various alcohols, he closed his eyes and fell asleep.

# 24

## About that Ally

Tam walked toward Sam's Place alone, lost in her own thoughts. As she passed the baseball field a cough disrupted her reverie. A short section of bleacher behind the batter's base partially hid the man who sat there. Tam continued to walk on by but someone called her name. The sky rained a spectacular orange and yellow display across the distant horizon as the elongated shadows of the evening dusk crept in somber silence over the scene. She stared at the figure who sat at the one end of the bleacher and tried to recognize him.

"Who are you?" she asked nervously. "What do you want?"

"Forgive me, Miss Clyde Walker. I didn't mean to frighten you, but we need to talk."

Tam moved closer to the figure who remained on the bleacher seat. A man of about forty, with a well-developed paunch and narrow shoulders, sat in quiet observance of her.

"I am Dr. Paul Shaw," he said.

Tam's eyes widened. "You're the scientist involved on a project in Hangar-3." She recognized him from the picture in his file.

"That's correct, Ma'rm." He spoke with a distinct British accent.

"Are you able to talk now?" she asked.

"Not here—perhaps in one of the dorm rooms—either mine or yours will do."

"Let's go to mine. It is closer to this end of the base," said Tam.

"If you don't mind going back on your own, Ma'rm, I'll follow in a little while—in case someone's watching. We have to be extremely careful."

"Are you being watched by security?"

"Yes, Ma'rm, but not all the time. They know I have had words with the project management and I suspect I'm under constant surveillance."

"You are talking about Robin Clandecker?"

"The same, Ma'rm."

"I'll see you in a little while, then." Tam turned and walked back to the dorm.

Several minutes later, Tam heard a soft knock on her door. She let Shaw into the room and motioned for him to sit in the chair at the desk while she parked herself on the bed.

"You're involved with a project that builds nano-robots, this much I already know. I also assume you know who I am?" asked Tam.

"Yes, Ma'rm. I know about you and Special Agent O'Malley."

"Were you contacted by the CIA?"

"No Ma'rm. I have another source of information. I believe you have already met the person I am speaking about," answered Shaw.

Tam looked confused. "I'm sorry. I don't think I've met your source—not that I recall."

"He's name is Maguilor, Ma'rm."

Tam recognized the name. "The strange being in Hangar-3?"

"The same, Ma'rm. He said you dropped in, so to speak, to see him a few evenings ago."

Tam could not believe her ears. "It's really true, then. Aliens have visited our planet. Maguilor told me he was the commander of an alien spacecraft, which the air force shot down many years ago."

'Yes, Ma'rm. In 1997, over the Arizona desert, near Phoenix." I heard Clandecker say that your FBI friend broke into the lower level through the vent system, but when I spoke to Maguilor he told me it was a woman who called herself Maria, but whose name was really Tammy Clyde Walker. I knew it had to be you."

"How did Maguilor know I work for the CIA?"

"These Beings have a very special intellect. They can read our thoughts. Maguilor's craft was shot down by the military and it crashed-landed near a compound run by some religious nut. The military consequently found the wreckage and took prisoners."

"What has happened to the others and where are they?"

They are living on the third level of Hangar-3."

"Have you been to level three?" asked Tam.

"Only Clandecker, General Watkins and some-one from the Pentagon—a five-star general, have clearance to go down there. I have never been past level two."

"I saw a type of clinic when I landed at level two, through the vent system."

"I work mostly in a lab situated on level one, Ma'rm. It's where we do all our experimentation and build nano-products for the project. There are four of us, which includes the medical staff. I also have clearance for level two, but only go down there occasionally."

I take it you've not been happy with what's taking place with this project?"

"No, Ma'rm. I suspect Clandecker is using our endeavors for something sinister. Whenever I tell him what parameters I'm using and what intended outcomes should be, he often tells me he requires a different perspective. I point out to him that the perspective he is looking for will change the end result."

"When you say, change the end result, what do you mean?"

"The result will be counterproductive to the intended outcome—in other words, unsafe for human application."

"—and let me guess—he tells you it's not for human application, or, it doesn't matter—right?"

"Correct Ma'rm."

"What happens on level three?" Tam asked.

"Maguilor told me there are more of his species down there. Only Clandecker, General Watkins and the Pentagon general really know all the details."
"Special Agent O'Malley should be back on the early morning flight. Will you be willing to meet with us and talk?"

"Depends on how closely I'm being watched," said Shaw.

Tam reached over and patted his knee. "Dr. Shaw—you must have heard that something terrible has happened in the small town of Hemlock. Over thirty people have died from a strange virus which left no trace of itself in their systems, and the victims all died from massive organ failure. I think you believe, as I do, that there is a strong correlation between the work you are doing and this catastrophe."

Dr. Shaw hung his head and stared at the floor for a few seconds. "I am having nightmares about it, Ma'rm."

"Then it's the most important thing in the world, that you speak with us and we put a stop to it."

He looked up and held her stare. "I have put my life at risk, Ma'rm—to be here. I want to help, but I'm also afraid of what they may do to me and my family."

"If we don't bring Clandecker and his cohorts to justice more people will die. We will do our best to protect you. I can get your family on a protection program through the CIA."
Shaw looked dubious but relented. "Let me know when you want to talk again and I'll make myself available. I have an ex-wife and a son, who lives with her. I would appreciate it if you could get them out of harm's way."

Tam smiled. "You're doing the right thing, Dr. Shaw. I will send word in the morning and CIA headquarters will take steps to protect your family."

"Thank you Ma'rm. I had better get back to my room." He stood and held out his hand. Tam opened the door and glanced in both directions. The hallway appeared to be empty. She nodded her head and Dr. Shaw left the room.

She closed the door, sat down at the desk and opened her laptop.

*

O'Malley looked at the image in the mirror. His face looked haggard and tired, eyes red and hair in disarray. He rubbed his chin and felt the rough stubble of beard as he weighed up the events of the previous evening.

Thoughts of the two strange men lingered on his mind. Where did they come from? How did they have so much knowledge about his affairs? The drain for the third level of Hangar-3 seemed a wonderful idea, and Clem Harris appeared to be an upfront sort of person, but since his conversation with the strangers, he doubted the plan's viability. Also on his mind, the unfortunate situation between himself and his wife, Janet, nagged at him. How would he make it up to his son? It appeared that his attempts to find fulfillment in life always ended up in the alienation of his family.

O'Malley shaved and dressed, then called for a taxi. Hunger would have to wait until he arrived at the Janet Terminal, where a light breakfast and coffee could be purchased. He looked forward to Tam's presence again. They would need to make a decision as to Harris's suggestion, and a new way would have to be found. A meeting with Dr. Paul Shaw might produce another avenue.

The twenty-minute flight seemed to take an eternity. O'Malley dozed on and off until the wheels touched down on Area 51's main runway. The jolt woke him out of his semi-conscious state and the airline hostess gave the usual rundown on safety, to stay in his seat until the aircraft came to a standstill. He looked at the small terminal building and saw Tam waving her hand. He waved back at her as the aircraft rolled to a stop and moved into position, to await the portable stairway.

A short time later O'Malley and Tam met up in front of the terminal building and embraced. "I've missed you so much," she complained.

"I couldn't wait to get back," he said. I have some interesting things to tell you."

They left the terminal and walked toward the dorms, arm in arm. A cammo-dude stood inside the terminal entrance and watched them walk away. He pulled the compact radio off his belt, keyed the mic and spoke a few words.

\*

Lieutenant Blake stretched over to the radio, which rested on the credenza behind him and grabbed the mic.

"You say he's arrived?"

"The dude's voice crackled back over the speaker. "Yeah, boss. His girlfriend has just met with him and they're walking off toward the dorms like two love-sick puppies."

Blake's eyes narrowed. "Keep an eye on their movements. I want to know who they speak to and where they go."

The voice crackled again. "I'll park outside the dorm and wait for them to leave, boss."

"Do that," ordered Blake. He turned to Captain Benson, who sat in the chair opposite. "O'Malley's back, we'll keep an eye on them. Is there anything else you require, Sir?"

"Make sure your men know not to let them out of their sight and report anything suspicious."

"They know what to do, Sir. What are your plans for today?"

Benson stood to leave. "Clandecker and I are driving over to Hemlock. We need to find out from Tobias if our secret is still intact. The sheriff has apparently been asking a lot of questions."

"They're eventually going to figure out what's really happened."

"I know, but the old man would prefer it to be later than sooner. Project Omega will hopefully be well on its way before anyone can point a finger at the military."

"I'm looking forward to our retirement," said Blake.

"An extremely well earned and luxurious one, no doubt."

Benson stopped at the office door. "Just make sure you take care of business."

# 25

## A heart to heart

Tam lay with her face on O'Malley's chest. She loved the feel of his firm pectoral muscles and the defined abs that formed a neat six-pack. Their love-making left her with a contentment she had not experienced in a long time.

"Did you see Janet and Steven?"

He shared the events of the previous evenings meeting with his wife and how strained the atmosphere had been.

She reached up a hand, pulled his face toward her upturned lips and kissed him gently.

"I'm sorry to have caused you this pain."

He lifted his head and stared down into her eyes. "You have not caused me any pain, my love. This turn of events has been a long time in coming."

"But still—it's a painful matter for you. I can tell you from experience it will get worse before it gets better."

"It's not Janet I'm worried about—it's Steve. He's at an impressionable age and will not understand any of these dynamics. He has been in the middle of our marriage war ever since Fallon died."

"Boys are always difficult to get through to. Raymond and I never had any children, fortunately. We just kind of drifted apart and then he had an affair."

"I'll have to learn from you," said O'Malley.

She lifted her head and kissed him, again. "What are you going to do when you get back to D.C.?"

"She says she is going to see a lawyer, so I guess I'll have to retain someone to handle the divorce."

"Are you sure that's what you want, Dillon?"

"I'm not sure, but I can't continue to live this way. Janet and I kind of keep each other in a state of conflict and its to do with my daughter's death. Neither of us can really move on."

"I know the feeling. It's a hard call, but eventually, you realize it's the only one that can be made in order to resolve the problem," said O'Malley.

"You intimated there were some interesting things to share about your stay in Vegas. How did your meeting with Clem Harris go?"

"It went very well, however, there is a caveat to the idea he shared."

O'Malley told her about the proposed entry plan shared by Clem Harris and how perfect it had seemed for their purpose.

"But then a twist to the story happened, which has left me undecided about Harris's intentions."

He told her about the two strange men who had apprehended him on the way back to the Strip and the warning they had given regarding Clem's proposal. Tam sat upright and stared at him.

"What did they look like?"

O'Malley described what he remembered and Tam gave a gasp of wonderment. "You have just described Maguilor."

O'Malley's jaw dropped. "That's the person they talked about. Now I remember your words when we met on level two that night—Maguilor is the alien you saw in the clinic."

Tam's eyes seemed to take on a vacant stare as she contemplated O'Malley's experience.

"You were met by two of the beings who were taken prisoner when the air force shot down that UFO in 1997. How on earth did they manage to escape the bunker without being detected?"

"They didn't tell me. Maybe Clandecker doesn't know what powers these creatures really possess."

Tam proceeded to tell O'Malley about her meeting with Dr. Shaw. "Paul told me Maguilor knew who I was—he has the ability to read minds."

"Now I understand how those two aliens knew all about my meeting with Clem Harris. They knew what he and I had discussed," said O'Malley.

Tam frowned. "If they can read minds and move about at will, I wonder why they don't escape from Area 51?"

"I remember one of them saying that they were not given any power in the situation. This may be because the clinic is keeping Maguilor alive. You mentioned he looked to be on his last legs."

"Maybe Paul knows. We need to make a plan to meet with him and find alternative access to the bunker."

*

Robin Clandecker and Captain Benson pulled up at the field hospital in Hemlock. Dr. Tobias, having returned from Vegas to close things down, greeted the men as they disembarked from Clandecker's truck.

"Can we talk?" asked Clandecker.

"Let's go to my tent,' said Tobias.

The three men walked through the empty marquee to the other end and out to the small tent, which served as the office.

"As you can see we're planning to move out of Hemlock. I assume it has been decided there will be no further runs made on the reservoir?"

"There will be no further dosing of the town's water supply. The old man has confirmed with E.M. Tech—there's no need for more tests. The product works perfectly," said Clandecker.

"I can attest to that. Our lab in Vegas has not been able to establish any link to the water. The residue has not led to any conclusions," retorted Tobias.

"We know how to build nano-products, Toby."

"You wanted to ask something?"

Clandecker nodded. "Has the sheriff mentioned anything more about the two government agents?"

"No, he hasn't, but Morty suspects something. He keeps asking me if we've worked out what that residue in the water is."

"You just keep stringing him along," said Benson.

Tobias pulled out a handkerchief and blew his nose. "As long as you can keep the FBI and CIA at bay we'll be fine."

*

Dr. Paul Shaw gave three raps on O'Malley's door. He looked furtively up and down the corridor but no one else appeared to be in the dormitory building. He slipped into the room as O'Malley stepped aside. Shaw looked nervously around the room but the only other person was Tam.

He greeted her with a nod of the head. "I don't have much time. I managed to slip Lieutenant Blake's goon, but he'll be looking for me."

"We won't detain you any longer than we have to, Dr. Shaw," said O'Malley.

Shaw sat down in the room's only chair while Tam and O'Malley sat on the bed.

"We'll come straight to the point," said O'Malley. "We need to gain access into Hangar-3. We were told of possible access through a floor drain in the third level but our mutual ally, Maguilor, sent a message that to use it would be very dangerous."

O'Malley shared his experience in Vegas with the two aliens. Dr. Shaw became excited and clapped his two hands together. "You met Mac One and Two? I've seen them in the clinic with Magailor from time to time. Clandecker allows them to visit on occasion. Not that he really has control of their coming and going."

"Where do Mac one and Two live?" asked Tam.

"The aliens are confined to the third level, Ma'rm. Clandecker has a hold on them because we are keeping Maguilor alive. He was seriously wounded in the UFO crash of 97, in the Arizona desert. Maguilor was the alien ship's commander and leader of their interstellar expedition."

"What will happen when he dies?" asked O'-Malley.

"I really don't know. I think the aliens are awaiting a visitation from their own kind. They don't know how long it will be before a rescue force arrives—it may not even be in our lifetime. Despite their advanced capabilities, the distances are just too great."

"What about a way into Hangar-3? Do you know of any access we could use to get in undetected?"

Dr. Shaw leaned back in the chair and gazed out of the window in contemplation of O'Malley's question.

"I think I know of a way. It will be dangerous but I believe we can pull it off. Every three days a truck enters the top level, to deliver a nano-organic catalyst, used in the manufacture of nano-robotic compounds. The catalyst is stored in a thick plastic bag, which is removed from the container when the product is required for processing. The empty containers are used to dispose of residues and precipitation, which build up over time, and need to be dumped, outside the base perimeter. I am in charge of all this."

"How big are the containers?" asked Tam.

One container will accommodate two people with a bit of a crush." said Shaw.

Tam turned to O'Malley. "We won't mind being crushed together for a short while, will we, my love?"

O'Malley chuckled. "I think I could put up with that—for a short while."

"I order containers of catalyst from E.M Technologies, which are stored in the warehouse behind the admin building for a night, or two. They're picked up and moved to Hangar-3 every third day. I have a few empties in the warehouse, which were not used for the dumping of waste product—these are usually sent back when too many accumulate."

"Are you sure there's no scrutiny of the containers on the way in?"

"There's no checkpoint between the warehouse and the bunker. The entrance security gate at Hangar-3 is automated, so nobody will check the product on the way in. The truck has a winch for offloading the containers onto dollies, which are then moved down in the elevator to a storage area on level two, next to the clinic. I oversee this process."

"It sounds do-able," said O'Malley. He turned to Tam. "Are you on board with this?"

"How will we get out?"

"The same way you got in," said Shaw.

"You said this takes place every three days?"

"There are places that one can hide on level two. I will be able to supply you with food and water once you're in there, but we'll have to be careful," said Shaw.

"We want to get into the third level. That's where Clandecker is setting up the final product, which we believe he is going to use for some upcoming catastrophic event."

Dr. Shaw stood, to take his leave. " I must go now."

"Just one more question. Do you have nay idea how we may get to the lowest level?"

The scientist moved to the door. "The elevator is the only link between the third and second levels. You'll have to organize some way of shorting the electrics—isn't that a specialized part of your training?"

Tam chuckled. "Amongst many other things. We'll figure it out. When do you want us at the warehouse?"

"Be there at 6:00 a.m. tomorrow morning. I'll meet you outside the back entrance. The transport still has to be arranged with the driver and I'll do that this afternoon. You'll be inside the bunker by 7:00 a.m."

After Dr. Shaw left Tam turned to O'Malley. "I wish there was a way we could get our firearms back."

"We won't need them while in the bunker. No one other than the security dudes carries firearms on the base and they don't have clearance for Hangar-3."

"I guess you're right, Dillon. It's the unknown factor on the third level that worries me, but we'll have to deal with whatever comes up. I'm going back to the office for the rest of the day—what are you going to do?"

"I'll be here in the room until dinner time. We can walk up to Sam's when you're finished with your work."

Tam kissed him gently on the lips. "What about later tonight."

"We have to get an early start tomorrow morning, so you'll need to behave yourself tonight."

She feigned a "hurt-feelings" look and left the room.

# 26

## Breaking in Again

At 6:00 a.m. the following morning O'Malley and Tam waited outside the back entrance to the warehouse behind the admin building. Five minutes later Dr. Shaw strolled around the corner and approached them.

"The security goon who keeps an eye on my movements will be waiting outside the dorm at 6:30 a.m. he always follows me to Hangar-3 so we don't have much time to get set up here. I have to get back to my room by at least 6:20, to leave for the bunker."

He opened the back entrance roll-up door and they moved into the small warehouse. Four containers stood on wooden pallets, ready for loading. Dr. Shaw pulled up an empty container from several which stood in the back corner of the building.

"Help me move this new container," he asked.

They moved one of the four new containers to the back corner and replaced it with the empty.

"Hop in," commanded the scientist. "Let's see how snugly the two of you can fit in. It will be a bit uncomfortable for while, but I'll rescue you when you're safely inside."

O'Malley got in first and sat down with his knees against his chest. Tam followed and sat next to him, but faced in the opposite direction. It was a tight squeeze.

"The lid has a few holes to allow air so you won't have to worry about suffocating," said Shaw.

'Thanks, that's very comforting," said Tam. We'll wait for you to set us free."

Shaw set the lid in place and sealed it with a thick adhesive tape similar to the other three containers.

"You okay in there?" he called.

"We're fine—see you inside," shouted O'Malley.

The scientist gave the container a salutary tap with his hand and left.

They waited another twenty minutes before they heard the sound of a truck pull up outside the warehouse. The door opened, followed by the sound of footsteps as the driver walked over to the forklift and started the engine. Ten seconds later

O'Malley and Tam felt the pallet being lifted and placed on the back of the truck. They couldn't see each other in the darkness of their trojan horse, but clasped hands for the comfort of mind. Each pallet contained two containers which were not strapped down and O'Malley hoped the driver would handle the load with care. The weight of the catalyst product far outweighed their combined mass making the container a bit unstable.

The transfer went off without a hitch and soon the truck pulled off in the direction of Hangar-3. Ten minutes later the driver brought the truck to a stop and they heard the bunker's entrance gate open. The truck moved off again and they were inside the Hangar. Everything had worked smoothly as Dr. Shaw said it would.

The truck journeyed a short way into the bunker and stopped.They heard the sound of voices and someone jumped onto the back to attach chains on each corner of the pallet, for offloading. They experienced the lift and sway sensation as the driver operated the winch. Moments later the pallet with its cargo were placed on a dolly for transfer into the elevator. Both Tam and O'Malley breathed huge sighs of relief but their journey was not yet over. The elevator took a few seconds to reach level two.

Dr. Shaw's voice floated through into the container. "We're nearly there, just hold on."

They felt forward movement for another two minutes before Shaw whispered again, "We're here. I'll let you out after I've closed the storeroom door."

The sound of a metal door being closed was followed by the removal of the adhesive tape around the lid, which then popped open. Tam clambered out first, and then O'Malley. They were in a storeroom of about twenty by thirty feet which contained an assortment of materials. The agents stretched their limbs, glad to be out of their temporary hiding place.

"You'll need to stay in this room until the coast is clear. I'll come and get you—don't worry, nobody else comes in here."

They acknowledged Shaw's instruction and sat down on a crate to wait for his return.

"You okay, love?" asked O'Malley.

"Just fine," she answered. "Being in such close quarters with you is always a pleasure."

An hour later the storeroom door opened and Shaw beckoned to them. "Everyone, except a medical doctor who stayed back to keep an eye on Maguilor has gone for breakfast, so we have the floor to ourselves—I made an excuse about some figures I needed to work on.

"Where is the doctor?" asked O'Malley.

"He sits in an office next to the clinic and keeps an eye on vital sign monitoring equipment."

"Would it be possible for us to see Maguilor?" asked Tam.

"It would be too dangerous and besides he sleeps most of the time. The doctor will know if he wakes up. You need to get down to level three as soon as you can. I saw Clandecker leave with the rest, so now would be a good time to move on it."

"Do you think we'll be able to find the other two aliens?—the one's who spoke to me in Vegas," asked O'Malley.

"Mac One and Two? I don't know."

"Why are they called Mac One and Two?" asked Tam.

"They're just the names the lab staff gave them. I don't know what their real names are."

"Do you think they have an allegiance to Clandecker?" asked O'Malley.

"Only because he holds the strings which keep their commander alive."

"Interesting. Do you know how many aliens were rescued from the original wreck?"" asked Tam.

"Only Clandecker, Watkins and the Pentagon general know how many. Maguilor and the two Macs are the only ones I've seen—the Macs are brought up to the clinic to cheer Maguilor up."

"So, there could be more than just the two Macs down there?"

"There could be," answered Shaw.

"We had better get going. Can I borrow a screwdriver and a short piece of electrical wire?" asked O'Malley.

Dr. Shaw removed a small canvas wrap, toolkit from a metal cabinet and handed it to O'Malley. "You should find this helpful. There are electrical supplies in the storeroom. Wait here."

He came back with a roll of electrical wire. "The electrician left this here over a month ago and never came back to get it—how much do you need?"

O'Malley opened the toolkit and removed a pair of cutters. He took the roll from Shaw and cut off two six-inch lengths. "That should be plenty," he said.

Dr. Shaw grabbed the remainder of the roll from O'Malley. "I'll distract the doctor while you slip past the clinic to the elevator."

They waited for Shaw to engage the medical doctor in conversation before moving out of the lab and along the tunnel to the elevator, where O'Malley went to work. He unscrewed the tiny fasteners which held the electronic control box plate in position and attached the wires to different places in the circuitry. The floor light flashed and the elevator doors opened. He removed the two wires and screwed the cover plate back into its position. They stepped into the elevator and he went to work on the inside electronics. Seconds later the doors closed and the elevator started to move downward.

Tam snuggled up to O'Malley as they waited. The cab stopped and the doors opened to reveal a brightly lit, empty hall.

"Let's go," said O'Malley. They slipped out of the elevator and walked down a wide corridor, listening for any sounds of life. They could hear the hum of the air conditioner against the backdrop of other motorized equipment. Ahead of them, a double set of doors appeared to halt their progress.

"Ready to see what level three's all about?" asked O'Malley.

Tam nodded and he cracked one of the doors open to give them their first look at what lay beyond. The large room held a variety of laboratory equipment. Five tall, vat-like structures lined a far wall, all of which were connected in parallel by 6-inch pipes with pressure control valves. On the main workbench stood a combination of clear glass tubes, pipettes, bowls and beakers, all a part of some elaborate chemical experiment. Two smaller benches contained rows of smaller glass containers, all filled with different colors of liquids.

O'Malley moved through the door with Tam close behind. They surveyed the scene with curiosity.

"Clandecker's workplace," said O'Malley.

Tam spotted a laptop, with flashing numbers and figures running in separate windows adjacent to one another. "This computer appears to be monitoring whatever process is on the go here," she said.

She moved up to the bench and scanned the keyboard. "let's see what else is on the hard drive."

Without interfering with the monitoring process Tam tapped away at the keys and produced a separate window which showed all the current files. One title caught her attention:

"OPERATION HEMLOCK."

She opened it and expressed her surprise. "I believe this may be what we're looking for."

O'Malley viewed the monitor screen and gave a low whistle.

"This is a comprehensive record showing the construction of a nano-robotic device which partners with liquids, to be absorbed into the organs of the body. It started in the 90's under Dr. P. Nelson and was eventually taken over by Robin Clandecker."

Tam scrolled down and a chart with the heading, "Hemlock daily water Consumption," revealed the quantities of nanoproduct required per liter of water in a confined system.

Tam leaned in closer to the screen. "This is a chart of Hemlock's water supply and the amount retained in the reservoir."

"This proves our point. The military poison the water supplies with organ destroying nano-bots. But, how did they introduce the bots?"

O'Malley thought for a second. "Sheriff Cranwell said he heard a vehicle race through town in the early hours of each morning before the deaths occurred. My guess is that someone from the military sneaked in under the cover of darkness and poured a solution containing the bots, into the reservoir."

"But there is no trace of anything in the water. Surely the bots would not all have been consumed—some would have been left after each event?" said Tam.

O'Malley frowned. "There was a residue, remember? No one could say for sure what it was. I think Clandecker and his scientists found a way for the bots to dissolve somehow—as we thought it might."

"If only we could download this data," murmured Tam.

O'Malley chuckled. "We can." He dug into his pocket and pulled out the flash drive which General Watkins had given him.

"You're such a smart fellow, O'Malley," said Tam. She inserted the drive into a USB port and downloaded the contents of each page.

"We have to find somewhere to hide—Clandecker will be back soon."

Tam pocketed the flash drive, closed the window down and left the monitoring process running. At the other end of the lab, another set of double doors closed off whatever remained of level three. O'Malley remembered the diagram Clem Harris had shown him of the elevation; it was quite extensive. They moved up to the doors which O'Malley opened with a push of his hands. The sight which met their eyes both shocked and terrified them at the same time.

# 27

## Clandecker and Shaw

With breakfast over Robin Clandecker returned to the bunker with the rest of the crew. In his company were two medics and three lab scientists. They entered through the security entrance, parked outside the office on level one. With an early start to work at 7:00 a.m. the eight o'clock breakfast ritual helped to break up the morning schedule, and they would all work until their coffee break at 11:00, with lunch at 1:00 p.m.

Clandecker enquired about Paul Shaw, but no one knew why he had missed breakfast. The group caught the elevator down to level two while Clandecker remained on the first level to have a chat with Shaw. The others dispersed to their various work stations while Clandecker went to look for his colleague. He found the scientist busy at a table in the lab.

"What's up, Paul? You missed breakfast."

Shaw knew Clandecker would ask questions. He was prepared and the answers came easily.

Their dislike for one another aggravated Clandecker, but he knew Paul Shaw could not be replaced so late in the project.

"I have found an anomaly in the attrition projections. It looks as though we might have a problem with self-eradication in the final batches."

Clandecker tilted his head and raised his eyebrows. "Are you sure?"

"That's the reason why I decided to check on the latest figures before the current batch reaches the optimum values for final processing."

The supervisor looked doubtful and shook his head. "I'm not sure I see the problem but carry on and let me know if it's going to be something which will hold us up."

Clandecker left the level-two lab and walked back to the elevator. He felt certain that Paul Shaw lied about the anomaly. Once down in his own lab he went to check on the monitoring process. As he stood in front of the monitor screen the angle of the screen struck him as odd—he knew this from the reflection of the overhead lights. Someone taller than he would need to adjust the angle to deflect the overhead light reflection. Clandecker became suspicious and his thoughts returned to Paul

Shaw. The aliens never interfered in the lab or any of the processes; it could only have been Shaw.

He felt conflicted, however, due to the fact that Shaw did not have a clearance for level three, which meant he did not have the special security card needed for use of the elevator between the levels. Still, the thought plagued him, that his subordinate might be involved. Could Shaw be in league with the two agents and if so, how would he get them into the facility? The third level floor drain, under constant vigil by Lieutenant Blake's men, could not have been used. O'Malley and Clyde Walker would have been caught the moment they tried to use it. Clem Harris's recent call about his meeting with O'Malley about a means of entry appeared to be the one the agents would certainly use.

It did not occur to Clandecker that an opportunity might be provided through the catalyst deliveries, but his mind would continue to work on the possibilities.

*

O'Malley and Tam stared in disbelief at the scene before them. A group of five, tall individuals sat at a table which appeared to have been special-ly made for them. The chairs upon which they sat were not regular chairs either. The aliens stopped their conversation and stared back at them. The two agents stepped into the room and allowed the doors to close behind them. The room in which they found themselves sported odd decorations on the walls and a large section of metal rested in the back area, against a wall. The section contained a strange insignia and what appeared to be writing, on it. The edges were jagged and burned with fire.

O'Malley and Tam continued to stare and could not find their voices. One individual from the group stood and attached a half mask over its lower face. The words spoken sounded digitalized with a small amount of inflection to convey tonal value.

"I see you finally made it into our domain, Special Agent O'Malley."

O'Malley recognized the being to be one of the two aliens who spoke with him in Vegas.

"Yes, and thanks to your warning we did not use the floor drain for entry," said O'Malley. His voice contained a measure of wonderment.

"Dr. Shaw found a way—I see, a catalyst container in your thoughts," said the alien.

O'Malley couldn't suppress a smile and wondered how any detail might be kept secret from the aliens.

"It is as you see. Can we trust you not to reveal our presence here to Dr. Clandecker?"

The alien placed a three fingered hand on the device over its mouth. "Please forgive this ponderous translating device. Unfortunately, our pallets and tongues do not facilitate the forming of words common to your language. We do, however, understand your language. I will remove it while I address my comrades."

He moved the mask upwards, off his mouth and spoke to the others. The words flowed in a click, clack melodic sound, almost as though the alien sang a melody. The group answered in the same click, clack song, with enthusiasm. The alien allowed his mask to slip back into place.

"Of course we will not reveal your presence, Special Agent. We must move further into our complex, however, because Lord Clandecker might come in and see you."

"Lord Clandecker?" asked Tam.

The alien focused on her for the first time. "He has given himself this title in order to impose his will on us. I will explain, Agent Clyde-Walker, but first, we should move to another area where you will be safe."

The alien pushed his chair back and motioned toward an exit in an adjacent wall. The group stood in unison and waited for O'Malley and Tam to follow on behind the leader. They walked through the door, down a long corridor and into another large room, which contained several beds. They saw several more beings on the beds, who lifted their heads to stare at O'Malley and Tam. They passed through the sleeping quarters, into a passageway and continued along until it ended in a smaller room.

The leader pointed to chairs and the two agents clambered up onto them. The Beings were tall and towered over O'Malley's six-foot frame. At a guess, he judged them, on an average to be at least seven foot, six inches in height.

"You may refer to me as Mac One," said the leader. He pointed to another of the beings, who had followed them in and said, "—and this is Mac Two. These are the names your people have given us."

With so many questions, Tam didn't know where to start.

"Tell us about yourselves. Where are you from and how did you come to be here."

"I will give you the shortened version, Agent Clyde-Walker."

"Please call me Tam."

The alien's expressed no facial emotion. The long, bedraggled hair rested on broad, bony shoulders and each individual's large set of eyes carried dark, black pupils framed against blood-red sclera. Two holes served as a nose and a thin, lipless slit, passed as a mouth. They all possessed the same characteristic of bulging temples and an elongated chin which turned upward at the point.

"As you please, Tam. We are an ancient race of beings in comparison to your species. Our home planet is fifty-four light years distant, in what you call the constellation of Pegasus. To cut a long story short our engineers have mastered the art of close to light-speed travel, a velocity to which you have not yet attained. We started out on an expedition to this area of the universe with five spacecraft, a total of fifty individuals, about one hundred Earth-years ago. When we arrived we parked over one of your large cities with the intention of making contact with your race. Your military, however, saw us a threat and attacked us, unprovoked. My craft, which Lord Clandecker calls Ac1, was shot down over a desert, not far from here."

O'Malley couldn't contain himself. "You must live a lot longer than we do. You have to be close to one hundred and fifty years old."

"Our lifespans are much longer than yours, and different, however, anatomically we are not that much different to you humans."

"You've been holed up in this bunker since 1997?" asked Tam.

"When our craft was shot down two of our number were killed in the crash and Maguilor, our commander, was badly injured. The military found us quickly and dragged everyone from the wreck. They managed to save Maguilor's life. He has been in and out of intensive care for many of your years. To answer your question, Tam, this has been our home ever since."

"What sort of agreement does Clandecker have with you?"

"We told him that our species would not forget us. I told Lord Clandecker, when he first joined us here at Area 51, our people will return—that our military prowess was far superior to that of Earth's."

"So, he agreed to allow you to live here in exchange for peace when your people return?"

"That is our agreement. We also helped with some small technological innovations, mostly in the medical field. We were unfortunately not able to help with your space travel because certain elements and principles, which drive our technology, do not exist here in your solar system."

"I guess Clandecker wouldn't agree to allow you free reign of the base, or into the outside world because the government would not agree to it."

"Your government will not allow us to live anywhere else—other than in this bunker. They say, if the presence of aliens is discovered, it will cause a worldwide panic. Your species is obsessed with war and violence. We do not want to contribute to that in any way."

"Yet you were able to meet with me in Vegas the other night," said O'Malley.

"We have not told Lord Clandecker we are able to bypass his security at will. But because of

Maguilor, we choose to stay here at the bunker—it's a safe zone for us."

"How did you and Mac Two get to Vegas? asked O'Malley.

"We are able to move extremely quickly on our long limbs. The journey on foot did not take us long and we do not get tired, like you humans do."

"How many of you are there in the sanctuary?" asked Tam.

"There are eight of us, which includes Maguilor, but unfortunately he is dying."

O'Malley wanted to know about Hemlock. "Has Clandecker learned anything from you in the area of nano-robotics?"

"Maguilor shared things he perhaps should not have. I see in your mind you are concerned about a project called Operation Hemlock. It is true he shared technology regarding the self-eradication factor of nanomedical robots. This was never meant for the harm of your people. It was after the fact that Lord Clandecker decided to make use of it that way. Hemlock was their test run. Their future plan is called operation Omega."

Tam stared at Mac One. "We saw something about that on Clandecker's computer. A lot of people are going to die."

"This is the reason we have made a decision to help you. We are, however, sworn to peace and we have not been given the power to harm Lord Clandecker."

"If we can get out of here with the information from his computer we'll be able to put a stop to it," said O'Malley.

An alien entered the room and bowed before Mac one. He appeared to have a message and spoke with rapid staccato in the click, clack language. Mac One listened and appeared to give an instruction in return, then turned back to O'Malley and Tam.

"Lord Clandecker has entered the stateroom and is asking questions. If he finds you he will kill you both and we will be powerless to stop it."

# 28

## O'Malley and Tam on Level three

Clandecker brooded over the possibility that someone might have gained access to the contents of his laptop. He thought of the few weaknesses in the bunker's security and how it might be possible for someone to gain undetected entrance to level three. It did not take him long to figure it out; catalyst deliveries. Dr. Paul Shaw did not care for his authority. The driver of the truck might not have known of stowaways in one of the catalyst containers, but someone of Shaw's caliber could have organized it.

Clandecker closed down his computer, removed a pistol from the bench drawer and walked to the elevator. The time for a showdown with his subordinate loomed. If O'Malley and Clyde-Walker gained entrance with Shaw's help the scientist would pay for it with his life. He took the elevator up to the first level and went straight to the laboratory. Paul Shaw, busy at the workbench and with his back turned to the entrance, did not see Clandecker enter.

\*

"Follow me," said Mac One. He set off down a corridor which made a gradual decline into the bowels of the bunker. They found themselves in a low-ceilinged space which carried all the pipework and hydro lines from the resident boiler and substation, which supplied all three levels with water and electrical power.

"If Lord Clandecker suspects you might have gained illegal entrance to the bunker he will look everywhere, and that includes down here."

"We'll take care of him," said Tam. "Don't worry about us."

"He is a very cunning and dangerous man, Tam —do not underestimate him," said the alien.

O'Malley spotted a tool crib next to the boiler structure and after a quick investigation came up with a large eighteen-inch wrench. "We'll be careful. Thanks for your help, Mac One."

"I will return to our stateroom. No doubt Lord Clandecker will want to talk to me. If he asks me whether I've seen you I will have to tell him the truth—our brains are wired for honesty. Let's hope his visit is not to do with you."

"We understand," said O'Malley.

The alien turned and strode back up the incline to the main floor.

"How different they are to us," said Tam. "They can take sides but with a brutal allegiance to the truth."

"Their attitude is certainly refreshing, although in this case, I would prefer Mac One to lie on our behalf."

"Their integrity is their highest value and one they keep to the death—so different to human beings," said Tam.

"We need to prepare for a visit from Clandecker. I didn't think of checking the lab drawers and closets for weapons—he may have a revolver hidden somewhere."

"There are quite a few places to hide in here, however, it may be better if we split up," said Tam. "I'll stand behind the boiler structure."

"Good, I'll hide over here by the substation. If he does come in you make a noise and attract him towards the boiler. I'll creep up behind him and use the wrench on his head."

"You say that with relish," she said.

"If you think of what he's responsible for then I don't see why there should be any leniency shown."

The two agents moved into their respective positions and waited.

*

Dr. Shaw heard a noise behind him and turned to see Clandecker at the entrance. "What are you looking for Robin?"

Clandecker glared at him. "Someone's been snooping around in my lab."

"Well, it's not me," said Shaw. He turned back to the bench to continue with his work.

"I know it wasn't you, but I think you know who it is."

Shaw turned again and held Clandecker's stare. "What are you talking about?"

"You didn't come for breakfast this morning because you were assisting those two agents to gain entrance to the bunker."

"You're hallucinating, Robin—now, bugger off and let me get on with my work."

Clandecker did not let up. "You used the catalyst delivery that came in the morning, didn't you?"

"You have to be joking, Clandecker. Why would I do such a thing?"

"Because you've never really been on board with this project. You found out about Operation Omega and Hemlock—you've always been too principled, Paul."

Clandecker pulled the revolver from his coat pocket. "I can't allow you, or those two law enforcement idiots, to jeopardize the program. You may know what Omega is but you don't know why we are doing it."

Paul Shaw turned to face Clandecker. "This is all hogwash and you know it, Robin. Please put the gun down."

"Not until you tell me the truth."

"Okay, okay. You're right. I helped them to get in but that's all. Now, put the gun down."

Clandecker pulled the trigger. Paul Shaw could not believe his eyes or ears when he heard the bark of the pistol and saw the gun jerk upward in Clandecker's hand. He toppled forward and crumpled to the floor. Clandecker moved over to him, bent down and turned the body over on its back. The sightless eyes stared up at the ceiling. No one else witnessed the incident as the others were all on a coffee break. He glanced up at the wall clock— 11:05 a.m.

He dragged Shaw's body into a small storeroom, adjacent to the lab and left it there. Minutes later he walked into the alien sanctuary and demanded to see Mac One. The alien came and sat down at the table and fitted on his translator mask. He could see by the look on the scientist's face that the presence of the agents was known to him.

"Where are the two humans? I know they had to have come in here."

"The two of whom you speak are in the building—they are in the utility area."

"Thank you, Mac One. These are two bad people who mean you harm, but I will see to it that they pay for meddling in our affairs."

Mac One viewed Clandecker without animosity. "As you, say, my Lord."

"We will continue to look after your leader and give him the best care possible, plus make sure you have all your needs met," said Clandecker. When your people come we will have eliminated all the ones who want only war with your species."

"As you say, my Lord."

"You do realize that Operation Omega is about preparing a peaceful transition of power to your species when they arrive to rescue you?"

"I understand, my Lord. We are fully committed to peace."

"Excellent. I will go and eradicate these two vermin who threaten that peace," said Clandecker. Our two species will live in harmony once we have dealt with those who oppose it."

"As you say, my Lord."

Clandecker stood and moved toward the corridor. Mac One continued to sit at the table but his large slanted eyes followed the scientist until he disappeared down the corridor.

*

Clandecker's footsteps echoed against the walls of the passageway as he made his way toward the utility section of the bunker. He arrived at the start of the walkway and softened his footfalls, with the pistol held at the ready. The area smelt dank with the moisture from the boiler. He knew the agents would be waiting for him. He also knew of the confiscation of their guns by General Watkins, which meant they would be unarmed. O'Malley could not have got a second weapon through security at the Janet Terminal in Vegas, a precaution taken by Watkins.

The background noise from the boiler and the substation echoed up the passageway toward him as he moved with caution down into the utility room. Clandecker stopped at the entrance and searched the visible area. Nothing appeared to be out of the ordinary. He held the weapon out in front of him and advanced further into the room.

He stopped before the boiler structure and shouted a command: "O'Malley, Clyde-Walker— come out with your hands up. I know you're both in here."

When he received no response he shouted out again. "You can't escape from the bunker. I'm armed and I will shoot if you try anything."

A sound came from the structure in front of him. He crept forward with the gun at the ready, his eyes glued to the pipework, which ran in and out of the boiler. The noise came from behind the structure. It came again but this time, from the other side of the boiler. He shouted another warning.

"Come out from behind there. If you don't I will start firing."

A sudden noise came from behind him. He swung around but saw no one. He became nervous as a scraping sound emanated from the boiler, and turned to confront it.

A voice said, "Please don't shoot—I'm coming out with my hands up."

Out of the shadows stepped Tam with her hands held high. Clandecker suspected a trap and on the detection of a movement behind, he turned. O'Malley threw the wrench and caught Clandecker across the chest with force. The scientist maintained his grasp on the pistol, but the force of the wrench knocked him over backward and he fell to the floor. In periphery vision, his eye caught Tam in the process of a forward lunge toward his position. The pistol came up and he fired off a quick shot at her, then turned to cover his rear. He saw O'Malley dive toward him and another shot rang out, but the bullet embedded itself in a nearby metal cabinet. In a split second, O'Malley landed on top of him. The special agent did not wait on introductions. He grabbed Clandecker's head between his hands and started to pound it against the concrete floor. Clandecker went out like a light.

O'Malley lay on top of the scientist's body and continued to pound the man's head until the body went limp. Then he remembered Tam; the sound of the first shot still rang in his ears. He looked over to where she lay and his heart froze. A second later he galvanized into action and jumped up to attend to her. She lay spread-eagled on the floor, her body motionless.

"Tam, wake up," he cried.

She did not respond. O'Malley placed his hand on her neck and felt the jugular. A slow throb of the blood pulsed beneath his fingertips. A voice sounded in the background.

# 29

## A Race against Time

"Are you okay, Special Agent O'Malley?"

Mac One knelt down beside him to look at the CIA agent's pallor. O'Malley looked up at the alien with tears in his eyes.

"Please, you must help me save her. She's still alive."

"We need to get her up to the clinic, said Mac One.

Mac Two and another alien appeared at their side. "We will carry her."

O'Malley looked over at Clandecker who lay unconscious on the concrete floor and pointed at the scientist.

"Do you have any rope or something I can use to secure this man?" The third alien stepped over to a metal closet against the one wall and rummaged around. He returned with a length of electrical flex and handed it to O'Malley.

"We are not permitted to inflict any harm on Lord Clandecker according to our code of conscience, however, you can tie him up yourself and we will place him in a safe place where he will be alone. I will tell those who remain to stay far away from him so that they do not hear him call out for help."

"Thank you, Mac One," said O'Malley. He grabbed the flex from the alien and proceeded to tie Clandecker's hands and feet, while the other two aliens lifted Tam between them, and made ready to cart her away. O'Malley kept his head. He dived into Clandecker's pockets and found the scientist's security card. They would need it for the elevator.

"Hurry," said O'Malley. "We must get her to the clinic as quickly as possible. Another two aliens appeared at the entrance to the utility room and Mac One ordered them to place Clandecker's unconscious body in a storeroom. A whole lot of click, clack passed between the aliens and O'Malley assumed instructions were given for everyone to stay well away from Clandecker. He understood that by their code they would be constrained to set the scientist free when he woke up and asked to be released. He would demand it of them.

O'Malley tied Clandecker up and made a motion for the aliens to take him away. Mac One and his two colleagues carried Tam through the entrance up the incline and into the corridor beyond. O'Malley picked up the pistol and followed at a run. The aliens were strong and their strides long. They ran ahead of the FBI agent, with one alien at each shoulder and the third at Tam's feet. O'Malley prayed she would hold on until they got her into the clinic. By the look of the wound, she could lose a lot of blood in a short time.

The Aliens burst through the sanctuary's doors and stopped in front of the elevator. O'Malley soon caught up and inserted the card into the scanner. The doors slid open, they all clambered in and the elevator zoomed up to the second level. O'Malley tried to use Tam's shirt to stem the blood flow from the wound. On the second level, they entered the tunnel from the elevator station and headed toward the clinic. O'Malley ran ahead and burst into the medical doctor's office. He pulled out his credentials and flashed it in the surprised doctor's face.

"FBI—I need your cooperation."

The doctor almost fell out of his stool with fright. He nodded his head with vigor and they ran into the clinic. The doctor summoned a medic from the lab to provide assistance as the aliens placed Tam's unconscious body on a bed, next to Maguilor's.

"Bullet wound in the chest," shouted O'Malley. The young doctor tore away the shirt and inspected the wound. He felt Tam's pulse and lifted her eyelids to check the pupils.

"Set up an IV line," he shouted. The medic responded and grabbed an IV bag from an adjacent mobile cabinet.

The doctor looked at O'Malley. "Who is this lady?"

O'Malley glared at him. She's a CIA agent and the love of my life, so you'd better save her."

His voice sounded harsh and strained. The doctor held his gaze for a second and then turned back to look at Tam.

"She'll be fine. The bullet passed through her upper chest, just below the collarbone. She needs blood, though."

He took a sample of the blood and handed it to the nurse. "Test this and tell me what the type is, please."

He turned to O'Malley. "We don't have too much blood on tap. I had to order in a week ago for our friend here." He pointed to Maguilor. "We have their blood type on hand—blood which the aliens donated in order to save their leader."

Maguilor positioned his translator and spoke for the first time. "I am glad you have decided to pay us a visit, Special Agent O'Malley."

The alien's knowledge of his name surprised O'Malley until he remembered the aliens could read thoughts.

"We couldn't stay away, Maguilor. There are things afoot here that our government would not agree with."

"Operation Omega, no doubt," said Maguilor.

"You have been aware of this operation?"

"For some time, now. I only picked up on it after sharing some vital information with Lord Clandecker, regarding his nano work. We do not agree with the purpose of Omega. I doubt whether your government even knows about it."

"You think this whole affair is known by only a few—a type of conspiracy?" asked O'Malley.

Maguilor started to cough and the doctor moved in to help him sit upright.

"You should not be talking, my friend," said the doctor.

Maguilor smiled at him. "The special agent should hear the truth, don't you think, Donald?"

The doctor looked puzzled. "What truth are you talking about, Maguilor?"

The alien gathered his thoughts. "The leaders of this secret project are not going to help mankind with their health problems. Omega has been developed by violent minds who want to make war and win at any cost. Omega is a weapon designed to bring the opposition into a state of fear, by causing millions of innocent deaths through controlled organ failure. These nanorobots are absorbed into the systems of ordinary people through what they eat, or drink. The robots are then activated remotely from a distant location."

The doctor's eyes opened wide. "I didn't know. Is that what this is all about?"

"I'm afraid so. But we aim to put a stop to it," said O'Malley.

The medic returned with Tam's blood sample results. "O negative, doc."

"That's my blood type. You can take as much from me as you need," said O'Malley.

The nurse set him up with a needle and transfer tube on a direct transfusion arrangement, for the blood to flow into an IV bag for Tam.

A short while later the doctor stopped the transfusion. "That's enough—she's going to be okay."

O'Malley relaxed and looked across at Maguilor. "So, Clandecker and his co-conspirators intend to take over countries who oppose our interests? How did they bring you into the picture?"

Maguilor moved the translator over his mouth again. "We were first approached after our incarceration here, to agree to a mutual truce and that we would be well cared for until our people returned for us. We did not come to your solar system to rule it, but to offer our technology and to live in peace with your species. Unfortunately, the air force shot our spacecraft down and we were captured. When Lord Clandecker arrived he told me he wanted to improve the health of all humans on the planet and I shared some of the medical technology from our ship's master computer. This technology included the healing of internal organs with nano-robotics, something which is old technology for us."

O'Malley rubbed the growing stubble on his chin. "You then detected a change of plan once they had acquired the technology?"

"I did. I sensed over the span of several meetings that they were planning a takeover of your government—to bring in a new world order. It has nothing to do with helping humanity or creating a peaceful transition when my species finally arrive to rescue us. General Van den Hoof, from your Pentagon, and Lord Clandecker, developed the concept between them, but then they had to bring others into it to help. I detected the growing selfishness of their thoughts."

"Who else has he brought to see you Maguilor?" asked O'Malley.

"There are at least five people who have come here at one time or another. One is a five-star general from the military headquarters in the place you call Washington D.C. and the second is General Watkins, the Groom Base commander. There was also a Captain, resident on the base and Lord Clandecker."

"Who is the fifth person?" O'Malley asked.

"Someone from a place close by—I can't remember his name."

"A small town close by—Hemlock?"

The conversation ended there as Tam woke up for the first time since the shooting.

"Where am I," she stammered.

"You're safe, honey. Clandecker fired on you when you charged at him. The bullet passed below the collarbone and out through your clavicle," said O'Malley. "You lost a lot of blood."

The doctor leaned over from the other side of the bed and looked into each eye. "How are feeling?"

"I'm thirsty," she said. "My mouth is so dry."

The medic rushed over to the sink and poured her a glass of cold water from the tap.

O'Malley realized that one member of the project team appeared to be missing. "Where's Dr. Shaw?"

The doctor looked at the medic. "He is usually in the lab on level one. I haven't seen him since the others returned from breakfast."

"I'll go up and see if I can find him," said the medic.

The doctor placed a hand on Tam's forehead to monitor her temperature. "You aren't running a fever—I'm sure you'll make a quick recovery. The back of your shoulder will a bit painful until it heals, though."

The medic returned ashen-faced. "I've just found Dr. Shaw. He's in the level one lab storage—dead."

O'Malley jumped up and stared at him. "Dead? How?"

The medic stammered and tried to regain his composure. "I think he was shot."

"Clandecker," said Tam. She shared the story of their entrance into the bunker. "Clandecker must have discovered we were in the facility and worked out how we got in."

O'Malley walked to a table and picked up Clandecker's pistol. "This is the gun he used to try and dispose of Tam and me down in the sanctuary."

"What are you going to do?" asked the doctor.

"I need to make a very important call. Do you have an outside line?" asked O'Malley.

"In my office. I phone out on occasion when we need stuff for the clinic," said the doctor.

Tam called O'Malley over to the bed and whispered into his ear. He approached her and inclined his ear to hear the message. He nodded and left the clinic for the office. The phone sat on the desk and he lifted the receiver to key in a number, given him by Tam. A voice spoke on the other end of the line. "Cactus Station."

O'Malley said four words. "The sun has set."

"We're on our way," said the operative.

He knew base security would monitor the outgoing calls and they would know where his short message emanated from, but they would not understand what it meant. Perhaps this would bring them in a hurry, or perhaps not. Tam shared that the CIA maintained a small contingency force, on standby at Rachel a small community close to the Extraterrestrial highway, about thirty miles away.

He pulled the flash drive from his pocket and inserted it into the doctor's laptop. A moment later the contents uploaded to an email, which he sent off. The FBI would know all the details of Clandecker's conspiracy.

His boss, James Ingram would inform the top brass at the Pentagon of the problem. O'Malley left the office and walked back to the clinic. Tam, now recovered, sat up to greet him.

"Did you get through?" she asked.

He smiled, nodded his head and sat down next to her.

"Your clash with Clandecker was a close thing," he said. "Two inches lower and that bullet would have ripped into your heart."

"But it didn't," she answered.

The aliens stood around Maguilor and chatted in their click, clack language. The alien appeared to be very weak, which solicited the doctor's concern. "I think you lot should return to your sanctuary," he said.

Mac One turned to O'Malley. "We will have to release Lord Clandecker if we return, and that could be awkward for you."

"Please wait on level two until our reinforcements arrive. Clandecker does not have his security card so he'll be stuck on level three. That's where I would prefer him to stay."

# 30

## Cactus Station

Lieutenant Blake found Captain Pearson in the gym.

"You must come quickly. I've just received a call from Clandecker. He's stuck in the bunker, on the third level. Those two agents managed to get in somehow and have discovered the alien sanctuary. He tried to apprehend them but they got the better of him and tied him up."

"Oh, Christ. I hope they haven't discovered any information on Omega."

"He's not sure but thinks they might have checked his laptop."

"Then we must assume the worst—where are the agents now?" asked Benson.

"They took Clandecker's security card and are probably back on the second level. Our monitoring team has just intercepted a call from the medical doctor's phone. It appears to be cryptic—something about the setting sun."

"Do they know where the call was made to?"

"They're working on it, as we speak."

Benson pulled a towel around his neck. "We need to tell the old man what's happened. He's going to blow ten gaskets this time."

Blake ran a hand through his crew cut. "I thought we had the agents covered—they were supposed to attempt an entry by the floor drain, according to Clem Harris, but it seems as though they managed to convince Paul Shaw to help them."

"Shaw? That rodent—I never liked him and I told Clandecker we should have got rid of him long ago."

"Clandecker has dealt with Shaw. He won't be telling anyone anything. We need to handle those two agents, though."

The two men charged out of the gym, jumped into Blake's four-by-four and headed for General Watkins's office.

\*

O'Malley sat beside Tam and stroked her hair. "How long do you think the contingency team will take to get here?"

"Rachel is not far away. I would say about thirty minutes," said Tam.

"They won't be in time if security picked up on my outgoing call."

"What are we going to do? General Watkins and his goons will be in here before we can get out. We can't hide down in the alien sanctuary, or anywhere on level two."

O'Malley turned to the doctor. "Is there any entrance into the hangar from level one?"

"It was rumored that a secret stairway was designed and installed long after the three levels were built, but I don't know where it is."

Maguilor coughed, opened his two large slanted eyes and moved the translator over his mouth. "I know where it is. I saw the plans for it in General Watkins's thoughts, several years ago."

O'Malley straightened up. "Do you know if it was ever built?"

"It may have been, but I don't recall him thinking about it on any subsequent visits."

"Is there any distinguishable area you could make out at the time?"

"I only remember seeing the entrance to a narrow stairway in a confined area—a small room, perhaps. The general was thinking about the drawing and its place in the actual potential area."

"A level one storeroom perhaps?" asked O'Malley.

The doctor chipped in. "There's a small storeroom close to the duty office, where they keep all the inventory records."

"I know which one it is. Blake's cammo-dudes threw me in there after my arrest, but I don't recall seeing a narrow stairway."

"It may have been hidden behind some crates," said the doctor.

"I'm going to take a quick look. I have Clandecker's security card for the elevator—I'll be back," said O'Malley.

He kissed Tam on the forehead and left the clinic at a run. Security might already be on their way to the bunker and could arrive at any time, but he needed to try. A short time later he approached the storeroom on level one, hopeful it would reveal the desired escape route. He opened the door and looked around. Cardboard boxes and wooden crates lay scattered over the floor and in one corner, against the wall stood a metal, double-doored cabinet. He placed both hands on the side of the cabinet, gave it a shove and it moved a few inches. He placed his shoulder against the side and shoved again, with all his might. The cabinet moved two feet and his heart gave a leap as he spied a metal door in the wall. He shoved harder and the cabinet offered up a full view of an entrance, about four foot high and two foot wide. He pulled on the door handle and it opened to reveal a narrow flight of stairs.

Satisfied, he closed the door and made his way back to the elevator.

*

CIA Special Agent John Durant replaced the phone on its receiver and shouted to his subordinates.

"We have a go. Come on, ladies—move your asses."

The four other men at "Cactus Station", a code name for their temporary appointment and situated on the outskirts of Rachel, looked up with expectant eyes. The time for sitting around, playing chess, reading magazines and drinking cups of coffee, appeared to be over.

"We have to move it—I assume the caller to be the FBI agent who is also assigned to the case. The code rendered could mean Tam is either occupied or injured."

They grabbed their weapons and charged out of the rented cottage, happy to be on the move again. The four-by-four's engine roared to life as Durant pressed the starter and selected first gear. "Hang on—this is going to be a rough ride."

The gravel road led to the main highway which serviced the county's rural area. They tore along the road under the darkening sky, with the sun well on its voyage, down, past the horizon. For a while, no one spoke, but as the lights of the base's perimeter loomed in the gloom, Durand confirmed his instructions.

"You've all been briefed on the layout of the Groom Lake base. Hangar-3 is our target and no one should be expecting us, except Tam and O'-Malley. We will order the checkpoint guards to open the boom. If they refuse I have orders to use force—we will need to quickly subdue them. There isn't a hell of a lot of security but they are armed. There will also be cammo-dudes, so watch out for them. Once we have breached the perimeter I will drive straight to Hangar-3. It's a normal-sized hangar on top of a bunker, which extends down two levels. There's an elevator control which we'll need to deal with, so be ready, Frank."

"Frank's short-circuit services at your command, my captain," said Frank.

"I've requested a backup from Creech Air Force base to be made available on request. It's a chopper with a CIA, S.W.A.T team of twelve, currently on maneuvers. They're combat ready and available if we need them."

The men were all in high spirits and ready for a fight. The CIA director's decision to involve a small extraction team for entry by road would prevent a possible retaliation by the Groom lake base commander, who might retaliate against an airborne invasion. The idea to extract agent Tam Clyde-Walker, if she got into trouble now also included Special Agent O'Malley of the FBI. The request came from the deputy director of the FBI, James Ingram.

The four-by-four hurtled toward the checkpoint and the two base guards looked up as they heard the powerful engine and the sounds of gravel under the tires. They watched as the vehicle slowed down and pulled up at the checkpoint boom. The driver leaned out of the window and flashed a badge at them. Two rifles poked out of the rear window to cover them.

"Put down your weapons. We are here by order of the United States Government."

Taken by surprise, both guards placed their assault weapons on the ground.

\*

Captain Benson and Lieutenant Blake sat in General Watkins's office and listened to the old man's tirade. He called them fools, idiots, and much worse. At the end of a full minute, he simmered down and became more rational.

"Okay. They're stuck in the bunker and can't escape. There's no vehicle with a gate modem, which means they can't get out through the main entrance. We have them trapped. I want you to take all the cammo-dudes you have on shift, Lieutenant, and get into the bunker. The agents must not leave the place alive—is that understood?"

"Understood, General. I won't let you down." You had better not, Lieutenant—if you do I'll make sure you're busted back to a private. You may go."

"You had better not, Lieutenant—if you do I'll make sure you're busted back to a private. You may go."

The lieutenant stood, saluted and left the office. The general eyed Captain Benson for a few seconds. "Your guys are not very competent, Ian. I want you to prepare for a visit from the CIA, and possibly the FBI. They're bound to send someone along to check on what's happened to their agents. Also, have Maguilor moved down to the sanctuary for a short time. I don't want Blake and his guard dogs to run amuck and seeing things they shouldn't. Make sure no one goes past level two—is that clear?"

Benson stood to leave. "I'll see to it, Sir." He threw in a quick salute and left. The late afternoon sun, now well below the horizon, framed the Groom Mountains in silhouette. An uneasy quietness settled over the base. The Captain headed toward his office with the intention of calling the guards at the checkpoint, to warn them of a possible visit by government law-enforcement officials. His ear picked up the sound of a vehicle on its approach to the base and he stopped to listen. No one ever visited the base by vehicle so late in the day. A sensation of foreboding swept over him and he started to run.

A moment later he heard the vehicle come to a stop at the perimeter. He burst into his office, picked up the phone and called the guards at the checkpoint, but got no answer. Without hesitation, he scurried out of the building, ran passed the dorms and photo lab to Security, where he hoped to find Lieutenant Blake. Two four-by-fours stood outside security's back entrance and as Benson arrived, the lieutenant accompanied by a group of security guards and cammo-dudes exited the facility.

"I think we may have company," shouted Benson.

"So soon?" answered Blake.

As the men clambered into the four-by-four a vehicle raced down from the checkpoint and onto the runway. It accelerated and headed for Hangar-3. No doubt remained in Benson's mind—they were under attack. Lieutenant Blake jumped behind the wheel of the first vehicle and roared off with a screech of tires. The Captain climbed into the second vehicle, which followed in hot pursuit.

*

Durant, with his team of four CIA combatants, reached Hangar-3 and parked their vehicle outside the huge hanger doors. To their left, they could see the ramp which declined toward a security gate. The special ops leader called for his technology expert.

"Frank, see if you can short-circuit that switch and get this gate to open."

The combatant moved to the control box situated adjacent to the gate. He reached into his backpack, pulled out a screwdriver and proceeded to force off the cover plate. A voice from the hangar doors interrupted them.

"Over here."

Ӝ

# 31

## Arrival of the Base's Security

Durant turned and spotted a man in the shadows of the hangar door. The stranger beckoned to them and disappeared back inside. Two four-by-fours raced along the runway toward them and Durant guessed it would be the arrival of the security team. He shouted to his subordinate. "Leave it, Frank—we have company."

Frank picked up his backpack and ran up the short incline to the hangar door, where he followed the rest of the team inside. Durant ordered two of his men to guard the entrance while he and the other two members of the team searched the interior of the structure.

"Keep that security detail at bay while we find out what's going on here,"

The lights switched on with a sudden intensity and they ducked for cover. There were large wooden crates scattered everywhere and toward the back of the building a whole conglomeration of burned and twisted metal. Durant tried to make out what it represented but could not define any particular shape. It looked like a crashed airliner and he supposed it to be the remains of a military craft.

A voice called out from behind a group of stacked crates. "Special Agent Durant? Over here."

Durant recognized her. "Tam? Thank God we found you. I thought we might have to break into the bunker. What's happened?"

A man stood behind Tam and held her upright. "This is Special Agent O'Malley of the FBI—we're on the same mission. Unfortunately, I've been shot, as you can see."

Durant nodded at O'Malley. A sound of rapid assault-rifle fire came from the entrance of the hangar. The CIA team leader turned and addressed one of his men. "Find out the strength of the attacking force and report back immediately."

The operative returned to the entrance and Durant focused on Tam again. "Is there any other way out of here?"

"Only back into the bunker. It's a secret connector which I believe only a few people know about, to the first underground level. It's called level one and there are two other levels below that."

The gunfire at the hangar entrance intensified and Durant looked back over his shoulder. "It sounds as though they have brought in reinforcements. We don't want to be trapped in here. Are there any other exits from the bunker?"

"Only the main entrance, which has a security gate. It's just to the left of this building."

"I saw it. We were going to enter there but someone called us from the hangar door."

"That was me," said O'Malley.

One of the men returned with concern written all over his face. "They have more men than us, Sir, and Simpson's been hit."

"How bad?" asked Durant.

"He can't hold his weapon but he can walk."

Durant looked at Tam and O'Malley. "We need to get out. Where is this hidden stairway?"

O'Malley motioned to one of Durant's men to help him support Tam and pointed to an office at the back of the building. "The stairway is very narrow—it's hidden inside a washroom closet."

Durant barked a command to the one remaining member of his team. "Get Bailey and Simpson, then follow us."

They moved off toward the back of the hangar with Tam supported by the two men on either side of her. Durant waited for the injured man and his colleague before he closed the metal door. One man would be posted at the bottom of the stairway to hold off anyone who found the stairs

The exit from the stairwell opened out into the storeroom below, the place of O'Malley's original incarceration.

With the team down on level one, O'Malley led the way to the elevator. He used Clandecker's security card and they headed for the clinic. Maguilor looked up at them from his bed and pulled the translator into position.

"Welcome back Special Agent O'Malley. And who are all these people with you?"

"Hello, Maguilor," said O'Malley. "This is a special team who have been sent to rescue Tam and me."

Durant and his men stared in horror at Maguilor.

"Is this..." began Durant, but words failed him.

"You'll have to forget everything you see here," said O'Malley. Welcome to Area 51's greatest secret. Neither you nor your men will be permitted to speak of this to anyone."

The elevator doors opened and they all looked at each other. The doctor reacted. "Someone has entered by the main entrance gate—do you have a plan?"

O'Malley shrugged his shoulders. "We'll have to fight it out—but not in here. I won't jeopardize Maguilor's safety."

"There is a large warehouse section down the tunnel, where the bunker ends. You'll find some cover in the warehouse. It will be difficult for anyone to get through the entrance without being picked off," said the doctor.

O'Malley thanked him and they left the clinic. The tunnel continued for another fifty yards to the end of the bunker and as they made their way with Tam still supported by O'Malley and another team member, two men stepped out of the elevator.

*

The sound of automatic gunfire startled the base commander. He grabbed his service revolver from a desk drawer, rushed out of the building and jumped into his Suburban. On his arrival at the hangar, he saw three four-by-fours parked outside, with Captain Benson and Lieutenant Blake, giving orders to their men.

Benson gave him a snappy salute as he approached. "A group of armed men held up the two checkpoint guards and forced their way in, General. They entered this building as we arrived and we got into a firefight. Then the shooting stopped and the insurgents literally disappeared. We've been in the building but they are nowhere to be seen."

"That's because they have escaped back into the bunker. There's a secret stairway hidden away in the washroom which no one is supposed to know about, but I guess they discovered it."

Blake tried to redeem the situation. "They were about to escape when they saw us coming. If they're in the bunker they'll be trapped."

The general considered the comment. "Is there still someone watching the floor drain from the third level?"

"Yes, General. They would be committing suicide to use it as an escape route, plus none of them have scuba equipment."

"Bring your men in, Blake, but you must re-main on level one until we say you can descend further. This is a highly classified area. We'll use the main entrance."

They left the hangar and ran around to the bunker entrance, where Benson used a hand-held modem to open the security gate. It took another few minutes for them to reach the elevator, where Benson and the general descended to level two while the others waited.

They stepped out onto level two and proceed along the tunnel to the clinic. Benson saw Durant at the far end of the tunnel. "They're here, General. Looks like they've slipped into the spares ware-house, to hide. We have them trapped.

"Close off the clinic so that no one can enter. I don't want any of Blake's men to see Maguilor." Captain Benson gave the doctor instructions to lock the clinic's door and ran back to the elevator. He used his security card and within minutes Blake's eight cammo-dudes stepped out onto level Two.

"They're in the warehouse at the far end of the tunnel. There's only one entrance, so be careful."

Blake nodded and gave his men the order to advance on the warehouse.

\*

Durant gave O'Malley the injured combatant's assault rifle. "We have limited ammo, so fire sparingly. They placed Tam and the injured operative at the back wall of the warehouse and made them both as comfortable as possible. O'Malley sat with Tam for a few seconds and consoled her.

"Don't worry. We'll get out of this and when we get back to D.C. I'm going to take you out to dinner."

"I'll hold you to that, FBI man. We can swap intelligence," she joked. O'Malley could see she was in pain. He kissed her on the forehead and then went to help the men set up a barricade.

O'Malley and the rest of the team waited several minutes before they heard a noise at the warehouse door. A cammo-dude stuck his head around the door for a quick look. Durant took a shot but missed and the man pulled himself to safety.

Another long wait made them wonder at the military's intentions until the voice of General Watkins floated through the door. "O'Malley? Are you there?"

"I'm here, General," shouted O'Malley.

"If you lay down your arms I promise not to fire on you. Come out and we can talk."

"With all due respect, General. I know what you and Clandecker are up to here at Area 51. You cannot allow me, or agent Clyde-Walker to escape. You'll have to come and get us."

"Sorry, you feel that way, O'Malley. I thought you FBI types were intelligent, however, it appears I was mistaken."

Another short silence followed. Two men burst through the door of the warehouse and fired their weapons on automatic. The bullets embedded themselves in the crates erected across the floor by O'Malley and the team. They fired back, but Watkins's men dived behind several boxes of supplies, positioned against the walls, on each side of the room. Two more men appeared at the entrance and started to fire on the barricade. Durant and O'Malley returned the fire in short bursts. They needed to spare their ammunition.

O'Malley heard a thunk as an object hit the ground close to his position. The atmosphere became murky with a thick, gray smoke—a teargas canister. Durant cast O'Malley a harrowed look.

They tried to see through the murkiness but their eyes started to sting and water. A few moments later O'Malley dropped his weapon and rubbed his eyes with the back of his hand. The fight ended without any further ado.

A boot landed with force on O'Malley's ribcage, followed by a blow to the head, which knocked him unconscious.

# 32

## Trapped

James Ingram, the deputy head of the FBI, read through the email, sent by O'Malley. He understood what the figures meant, and coupled with the knowledge of the Hemlock deaths, he grasped the enormity of project Omega. The recent call from his counterpart in the CIA confirmed their concern, with regard to some of the projects at the base. He also confirmed the appointment of agent Tammy Clyde Walker. With the murder of the adjutant and the two missing scientists, General Watkins's leadership came under scrutiny, but when he called Ingram for help focus fell on a few of his subordinates. These included Clandecker and Captain Benson.

O'Malley's experience, however, proved that the general and certain staff members were up to no good. The information from Clandecker's computer prompted a call to the White House. He knew O'Malley and the CIA agent would be in imminent danger if they were caught. Information gleaned by O'Malley suggested that the general, his chief scientist and a member of the Joint Chiefs of Staff, at the Pentagon, were all involved in a possible breach of trust.

Ingram shared O'Malley's email and its contents with his CIA counterpart. He suggested the setup of a team to invade the base, extract the agents and arrest the conspirators at the same time. The deputy head of the CIA confirmed such a team already existed and they would be glad to pull O'Malley out, along with their own operative, when the time came.

Ingram contacted the White House to confirm what he knew and asked the president to issue a directive to Watkins, with an order to stand down. A CIA backup team waited at Creech Air Force Base in California should they be needed.

*

O'Malley awoke in the darkness of a room. His eyes and head hurt from the effects of the tear gas and his ribs were painful from the kick. The cammo-dudes did not, however, cuff any of his limbs and he sat up to clear his head. A pungent smell from the toxins in the gas permeated the stale, dank air which lacked circulation. He waited a short while for his eyes to adjust enough to see some vague outlines. Light seeped through the bottom of a door, and shapes in the room began to appear out of the gloom.

O'Malley's first constructive thoughts centered on Tam's condition. What might their captors have done with her? The gunshot wound would need attention. He tried to move, but every muscle and joint hurt, another legacy of the toxic gas used by the military. With slow deliberation, he stood up and strained his eyesight for any signs of the others. Forms on the floor appeared in the gloom and he made out the bodies of the CIA operatives strewn around him, like discarded blankets. It would appear their captors did not remove them from the warehouse and he could make out the crates and boxes of the make-shift barrier.

He called out Tam's name but received no response. One of the operatives started to groan as he regained consciousness and O'Malley moved toward the stricken man, to find Durant, who clutched his head in pain.

"It will go away," said O'Malley.

Durant jerked his head upward and peered through the gloom at the FBI agent. "Where are we?" he murmured.

"We're still in the warehouse—I haven't tried the door, but we must assume it to be locked."

"How are the others?" asked Durant.

"We need to check on them. Let me help you up."

O'Malley extended a hand beneath Durant's arm and helped him to stand. They both felt light headed, but after a few moments, the sensation passed. With her back still against the back wall, Tam lay in her original position, with head slumped over onto a shoulder. O'Malley felt her pulse to determine proof of life. The weak, but consistent throb which pulsed against the tips of his fingers, brought an instant relief. They checked on the injured Simpson, who stirred as Durant touched his shoulder, as did the other three CIA operatives.

"They're probably deciding what to do with us," said Durant.

O'Malley sat down next to Tam. "We have to figure a way out of here."

Durant walked to the door and tried the bolt mechanism. "It's definitely locked. I wish I had called for backup while I was still in the clinic. I thought we would be able to fight our way out. The agency would have scrambled their choppers, each with a dozen men, to invade the base and extract all of us."

"Where are they stationed," asked O'Malley.

"Creech Air Force Base. It's near Indian Springs on the 95—approximately 45 miles away. It would have only taken about ten minutes to get here."

"Wouldn't General Watkins scramble his Hawk security choppers if the CIA mounted an airborne rescue?" asked O'Malley.

"He probably would, but I think the CIA's Creech-based choppers are more heavily armed and it would be a losing battle for the Hawks."

"Don't blame yourself, Durant. I also thought it would be better for us to fight our way out—we had the weapons. No one counted on them using a toxic teargas, though."

Tam stirred with a groan and O'Malley took her head in his hands. "Wake up, my love."

She opened her eyes and reached up a hand to caress his cheek. "I thought I was dead."

O'Malley explained their position. "We just have to wait and see what they do."

She managed a weak smile and then closed her eyes.

The door's bolt mechanism rattled and slid back. A figure stepped into the room and the lights came on with a blinding brilliance that hurt the captive's eyes. A cammo-dude with a semi-automatic in his hands stood and glared at them.

"The General has ordered me to bring you up to the hangar." The man, a rough desert soldier in his fifties, motioned them to stand to their feet.

"What's he going to do with us?" asked Durant.

"I don't know. I just obey orders," said the dude.

Another cammo-dude entered the room and stood to one side while O'Malley and Durant lifted Tam to her feet and supported her weight between them. Two of the other CIA operatives helped the injured Simpson to his feet and they moved out of the warehouse into the tunnel. The first dude moved on ahead while the other brought up the rear and the group walked past the clinic to the elevator. O'Malley noticed the clinic doors were closed and saw no signs of the doctor or Maguilor.

They reached the elevator and one of the dudes swiped a security clearance card. On level one the group stepped out and walked down to the main entrance gate. Both Tam and Simpson struggled to place one foot in front of the other and but for the assistance rendered by their comrades, would not have been able to carry on.

The cooler night air hit them as they marched out of the main entrance and up the ramp to the runway. The dude in front turned at the top of the incline and headed for the open doors of Hangar 3. The lights inside the hanger were duller than the tunnel and it took a slight adjustment for them to focus on the three figures in the middle of the hanger floor.

General Watkins, Captain Benson, and Lieutenant Blake awaited them.

The group stopped in front of the three men and waited for General Watkins to address them.

"It appears you've stumbled on a secret project which is not for the unauthorized. You have meddled in the base's affairs and your consequent discovery of Operation Omega has forced my hand."

"If by unauthorized you include the White House and Joint Chiefs of the Pentagon, then you're doing something for which you have no clearance," said O'Malley.

"Your interpretation of authorization is noted, O'Malley, however, once we prove the success of Omega, the authorities you mentioned will be quite willing to go along with it."

"You have murdered a whole group of innocent people, General. I can't see the authorities accepting the cost."

"If you mean a few sensation seekers from Hemlock, then the cost is justified in lieu of Omega's advantages, but I'm not going to argue the point with you. It pains me to add a few more deaths to the final cost, however, your presence is a danger to the operation."

The general turned to Lieutenant Blake. "See to the execution of these people, lieutenant."

Blake saluted and stepped forward. He called to the rest of his cammo-dudes to join the two already present. They all carried assault rifles and came to a stiff attention, guns at the ready. Watkins and Benson walked around the captives and made for the doors of the hangar. Blake gave the order for the men to raise their weapons.

O'Malley embraced Tam and tried to shield her from the salvo of bullets about to come their way. His final thoughts focused on his family. Blake told his men to take aim. The CIA operatives stared with vacant eyes and waited. Blake hung on to the order to fire. He wanted to create a climax which he and his men would remember in the performance of their first execution. Interminable seconds passed as each group waited. The cammo's waited for the final order to be given and the captives, each to take their final breath.

A volley of shots rang out and reverberated against the inner walls of the hangar. Tam cried out in fear and O'Malley gasped, but no one in the group fell. Instead, each witnessed the cammo-dudes fall, one by one. Their weapons fell to the ground with a clatter and bodies lay in agony in the throes of death. The captives could not believe their eyes.

A uniformed figure ran into the hangar and went straight to Durant. The two men embraced and then observed each other in wonderment.

Durant turned to O'Malley. "Meet my brother."

O'Malley almost did a double take. The two men were identical twins.

"You arrived in the nick of time," said Durant.

"We couldn't have timed it better. The boss changed the plan and we didn't land on the airfield. We came as soon as we got the message, but had to land two miles away, in the middle of the desert. It took us ten minutes to jog the distance with our packs and weapons," said Durant's brother.

Tam greeted the operative by name. "Glad you could make it," she said. For a moment I thought we were done for."

Durant's brother laughed. "I'll try not cut it so fine in the future. We've taken custody of the general and his two subordinates.

Durant remembered an important detail. "Who called you? I was supposed to do that but never got the chance. No one else had the number or the code."

"I got a call on a landline, from a medical doctor, who claimed to be working on a black project at area 51, in Hangar-3. He told me you guys were in danger and that this was the number he had to call."

O'Malley couldn't believe his ears. "We know who the doctor is but how did he get the number?"

Durant's brother shrugged. "He said someone by the name of Maguilor gave it to him. Do you know the person at all?"

O'Malley and Durant looked at each other and then, as understanding dawned, O'Malley laughed. "He's a real cool dude, but I can't exactly talk about him," said O'Malley. "I'll fill you in later, Durant."

Durant raised his eyebrows, "I think I get your drift."

"There is one last thing we need to tie up," said O'Malley. "Can you get me over the town of Hemlock?"

Durant's brother nodded. "Just tell me where it is and I'll see you get a ride in one of the choppers."

# 33

## A Shock for the Sheriff

The flight to Hemlock took about five minutes. The moonlight made the night's flight conditions easy and O'Malley instructed the pilot to land on the sports field. The chopper did not go unnoticed by the town's sheriff, who jumped into his truck and raced over to the field, while O'Malley and Durant walked toward the town.

"Do you guys need a ride?" asked the sheriff.

O'Malley introduced Durant. "We need to talk, Morty."

"I've got coffee at the station," said the sheriff. "We can talk there."

Mortimer Cranwell parked outside the station and they walked into the tiny office. He poured some bottled water into the coffeemaker and set up three mugs.

"What brings the FBI and CIA back to my office?"

O'Malley flinched. "It's good news, and not such good news, Morty."

He proceeded to tell the sheriff about the discovery of Operation Omega and how the town's people came to be poisoned. He didn't mention the alien presence but shared who the real culprits were.

"So this project Omega started with an experiment for a newly discovered biological weapon which involves nano-robotics?" asked the sheriff.

"Hemlock became the test site for it. The general thought the town might be dispensable due to the security risk the UFO and sensation seekers posed to the secret projects at the base."

"It's good of you to share this with me—I'll let Charles know," said the sheriff.

O'Malley grimaced. "I have a question for you, Morty. Your brother is the mayor, right?"

"You might say he runs the town's affairs," answered the sheriff.

"To your knowledge is there anything in Hemlock's future which might jeopardize your family's standing or ownership of the farm?"

"Not that I know of," said Mortimer.

Durant took over. "Sheriff, we know that your brother has been in negotiation with a Pentagon general regarding your town with all its businesses. The mineral mine is also running out and your brother has borrowed heavily from the bank to keep it going. The CIA has been collecting intelligence regarding this for several months now."

Mortimer Cranwell looked shocked. "Charles always told me the businesses were doing well. What are you saying?"

O'Malley recalled his conversation with Maguilor, the reader of minds, and gave a nervous cough. "Morty—you saved my life and Tams. We owe you a great deal, but there is some news I must break to you about your brother, Charles. We have it on good authority that he has met, on many occasions, with General Watkins and a general from the Pentagon. Both these men are involved up to their eyeballs in Omega. Charles has been seen inside Hangar-3 where the project has been on the go for a number of years.

The sheriff sat motionlessly and tried to take in the enormity of O'Malley's words. He made a final effort to come to grips with the truth.

"You're saying my brother has been collaborating with these generals to further the ends of this Omega project—and that he knew the cause of Hemlocks tragedy, but didn't say anything because he had made a personal contribution to it?"

Durant leaned forward in his chair. "Charles must have realized a long time ago that the town, with its failing mine, would eventually go bankrupt. He inspired the UFO business, didn't he?"

The sheriff nodded his head. "I didn't know the town's financials were that bad."

"He must have made a deal with the generals. They would buy up Hemlock and incorporate it into area 51's testing zone. Your family would be paid out a certain sum for the farm, but all the businesses would have to go bankrupt."

The sheriff, numbed by the accusations against his brother, buried his face in his hands.

O'Malley got up out of his chair and placed his hand on Mortimer's shoulder. "We believe you to be innocent in all this, Morty. Tam and I will testify how you saved us from those cammo-dudes. No one involved in Omega would have done that. Where is your brother at the moment?"

"He'll be at home," murmured the sheriff.

"Let's go and confront him then," said Durant. They left the station in the sheriff's truck and headed for Charles Cranwell's home.

*

O'Malley and Tam sat on a bench in Lafayette Park. D.C. His one arm draped her shoulder and she held his other hand in her own.

"Do you believe in aliens." she asked.

He answered her question with one of his own. "Do you?"

"I can honestly say that my life was saved by an alien."

He thought about her comment. "You're right. If Maguilor had not read Durant's mind when we met for those few brief moments before the cam-mo-dudes attacked us, we would both be dead."

"I'm still amazed that he was able to do that—as though he was looking for a way out for us."

"I think he had his eye on you, my love," said O'Malley.

She gave him a mock jab in the ribs. He winced.

"Sorry—I forgot your ribs were still sore."

"It's okay. I believe you asked your director if you could return to the base and see Maguilor for one last time. What did he say?" asked O'Malley.

She smiled. "He said it would be impossible because aliens do not exist at the base."

"And what did you say," asked O'Malley.

"I asked him if that was his official answer, and he said, yes."

"And unofficially?"

"The new base commander would never allow it—officially, or unofficially."

"I see. That's a great pity. I think Maguilor will soon die and we will never see him again."

"I will always remember his huge slanted eyes and his friendly manner," she said.

"Maybe Mac One and Two will visit us unofficially some time?"

"Who knows the mind of an alien—they certainly know ours."

O'Malley chuckled. "I hope they get to go home one day. It was a great privilege for us to have met with them."

Tam nodded her agreement.

"This would be a good time for me to ask a question," said O'Malley.

"Shoot," she said.

"You know I love you. When my divorce is through, will you marry me?"

She looked up into his eyes. "Officially or unofficially," she asked.

"Definitely official," he answered.

"I think I could make an arrangement." She lifted her lips to his.

Җ

# 34

### EPILOGUE

When General Van den Hoof of the Pentagon approached Robin Clandecker to take over the nano project, he offered the scientist a tidy sum to develop a nanorobotic system, which could destroy a complete population by poisoning its water supply, and thereby render an enemy powerless. Countries opposed to American ideals could be brought to heel by such a weapon.

A short time after that Dr. Robin Clandecker developed a self-eradicating nano-material, which would leave no trace of its presence after the fact. He gave credit to Maguilor's knowledge of nano-robotics, with first intentions of a robot which could attack tumors and growths. Clandecker in conjunction with Van den Hoof later saw the opportunity for the Omega weapon but knew the White House would never agree to the development of such a diabolical scheme, even if it could render countries impotent of resistance. The project, classified as top secret, remained unnoticed until the death of the base's adjutant.

General Watkins, the base commander was credited with the introduction of General Van den Hoof to Project Omega, and also the first to suggest Hemlock as a trial run for the weapon. He maintained that the town's presence always constituted a thorn in the military's side and if it could be shut down, there would be less opportunity for people to get close to the secret facility. The presence of the aliens provided another reason why Hemlock, the closest town to the base, should be eliminated.

The resourceful aliens, who took care of themselves required only water and flour, which they harnessed to provide all their life-sustaining needs. They were given wood, steel, and certain textile components to manufacture all internal accommodation requirements and seldom ever asked for anything else. They even made their own clothes.

Their most endearing value rested in the practice of total honesty. Promises were kept to death and agreements would never be broken. Their philosophy of life remained pragmatic and simple—stay true to the core values of society.

\*\*\*

AUTHORS NOTE:

There is no proof that aliens or UFO's exist at Area 51. The government has denied to this day, that a UFO crashed in the desert on the 13th of March, 1997. There is, however, much evidence to corroborate the belief that something dramatic took place on that night. The "Phoenix lights" incident is the most documented sighting of all time and there are many eye witnesses to the actual event. The strange arrangement of the lights created the impression of one large ship or several in a formation. The incident remains a mystery to this present day.

## More Books by Colin Setterfield

The Helium-3 Conspiracy

Love Sweat tears

*The A-Mortal Gene

*The habitat Relocation Project

*The Beautiful Planet

The Memory Hunter. Special Agent O'
    Malley

Merlin's War.   Special Agent O'Malley

Operation Terra Firma: Special Agent
   O'Malley

* Trilogy